ACKNOWLEDGEMENTS

I wish to recognize my greatest love, Brownie for coming to my rescue and for all the girls & young women that he rescued in his tenure to protect, comfort, understand, and ride like hell to a grand finish. He was always ready to carry the day no matter what it took: a perfect life of service. This little collection is his reward, his legacy, his Pulitzer Prize.

Brownie and I want to personally thank the cast of characters: Mary Ellen Treadwell, Yancy, Dash, Jasper, the two Shoshone Indian men, the Pony Express, Jimmy Stewart, Barbara Stanwyck, Glenn Ford, Richard Boone, Rory Calhoun, Viggo Mortensen, Russell Crowe, Clint Eastwood, Pie, Misty Girl, Tenny, Rafter, TJ, Honey, Midnight, Rate, Sam Elliot, Sam Peckinpah, the American Indians protecting their reservation, Grandmother Kit, Madison, Clipper, Mother Elizabeth, Ruth the Elder, Ronnie Stout, Irma Brighton, Kay,

Charlie, Mother Maude, Father Charles, Aunt Gertie, Margie Sterling, Clarissa Pinkola Estes, Catherine Sterling (Mother), Chandler Sterling (father), Beth Sterling, Pearl (my Toyota), the skeleton rider and his horse, the oyster, the Pearl, the Lady in Blue, the mackerels and jelly fish, my sister Lu, daughter Ann, & Margie's daughter Meghan.

And especially for the encouragement and support from my husband John, sisters Lu & Star Sterling, children Ann Clark, Joe Clark, Becca Rose Laird, and Levi Laird, Don & Jim McCloud (literary & creative writing teachers), Summer Graef (literary partner, writer, and inspiration), Sharon Kehoe (eternal writer, dearest Anam Cara friend), Julie Fodor (undying forever friend), Matti Sand (fellow writer & believer extraordinaire), Wanda Kuhl (friend, author & publishing teacher), Rebecca Rod (artist, writer, & excellent friend), Elizabeth Sloan (fellow author and workshop creator), Lumin (poet, technology), Jeanne Kyle (art), Talon Tuxill (book cover), the Big Sky Sisters, and all my listeners and Brownie lovers (you all know who you are!).

Let's ride...

Ride Mary Ellen, Ride

Dedicated to Bonnie Mary Ellen Treadwell McCarroll

The Treadwell Ranch was tucked up against a draw in High Valley, Idaho, just northwest of Boise. Mary Ellen Treadwell was turning a corner on seventeen years old in January of 1860. She'd been born a roughneck at least that was what her mother called her, disapproving of her early interest in horses and spending time with the ranch hands. Ma inevitably had to go looking for her after finding her missing toddler from her nap-bed.

It wasn't unusual to find her standing on the bottom rung of the corral watching a hand break a mustang. Once, as Ma saw her do just that and ran to her daughter, Mary Ellen climbed through the railing and stood laughing at the cowboy exiting the horse, six feet in the air! Ma screamed as he landed in the muddy quagmire of horse hoof ruts. The tough little mustang was wild with emotion bucking like the man was still on his back. When he realized he was free of him, he began running around the corral. Each time he got to the child, he did a little back kick even though he couldn't figure her out, and she was so small he kept kicking too high to hit her.

Granddad saw Mary Ellen in the corral and launched himself over the side where she was clapping and laughing. He swooped in like a red-tailed hawk and scooped her up. When he got her to the other side he just yelled at Ma telling her she needed to tie Mary Ellen into her bed, and "Never take your eyes off her!! Do you hear me Margaret?"

Ma choked and said defensively, "Well Pa, you try and watch her all the time! I got work to do too!" From the kitchen, she saw black smoke swirl out under the door.

"For the love of God, now my bread is burning!

This was Mary Ellen, always, and I mean always getting in the mix.

At sixteen and three-quarters Mary Ellen had grown up on the ranch. Hers was an exciting life of catching mustangs which was much more about outsmarting them than chasing them down. You had to be extremely skilled with a rope to make a catch, and often catching a wild mustang by rope wasn't the most successful. The chase was never predictable. First of all, the horse ridden would be best off being a mustang itself as other horses lacked the genetic makeup it took to keep up in the wild terrain. It was just risky for the sake of having a good domestic Thoroughbred or Morgan break a leg or to misjudge a ravine to end up in a world of hurt. And a wild mustang's hooves were tough and durable, much more so than non-feral horses, having spent generations adapting to high desert and rocky soil conditions.

Rather than chase mustangs on end forever and never catch one, mustangers figured out how to trap them over time: build a corral around a water source and for about a year let the horses use it without threat, track and watch the herds until the appointed time, then wait for action.

Now, this was how Mary Ellen got Brownie, her brilliant and tough little mustang that defined her in so many ways. He accidentally got caught one day after he and a few fellows found oats spilled heavily on the ground inside the corral. As soon as the horses were indulging in the delicious oats, Curley, a ranch hand at the time just closed the gate on them.

Free is the optimal word for a mustang; *freedom means no borders; no bits; no task masters, just independent freedom.* If they were struck by lightening in an open meadow during a thunderstorm it was their own nature that took them out. It was up to no one but their own habits, their own character and their own providence that determined their life or death. They were wanted by every human: Indian and white alike and now they were the only desirable horse for the Pony Express!

One afternoon, Mary Ellen was just returning from her mountain ride when she saw Granddad waving her in. He told her to put Brownie up and meet him at the house.

She unsaddled her horse and let him out into the inner pasture where he could munch the July grasses. As she hung the bridle up in the barn and swung her saddle onto the stump, she turned to see her Granddad standing with one foot propped on the porch railing. He'd just struck a match on the bottom of his boot to light a fat little half-smoked cigar. The smoke beckoned her out of the barn and across the hard pan yard.

Granddad, Yancy E. Treadwell, the first, was handsome as much as he was worn. He was of medium build with muscles like a well-formed greyhound, delicate, sinewy, and of no-nonsense. His Stetson sat tipped back above his hairline and was nestled on a head of graying hair that looked like a bird's nest peaking out. Mary Ellen loved him for good reason. She never knew life without him.

"Hey, Yancy," she piped up. She'd been calling him Yancy for about a year now and he never corrected her, even though her mother yammered on as to how disrespectful she thought it was.

"All right Mary Ellen, we've got some business to talk about. I just got word from a Major Solomon from the Army about selling some of our mustangs for the Pony Express, have you heard of it?"

"Sure Yancy, I heard of it." We're kind of north a ways to be gettin' our horses down to the route aren't we?"

Yancy tugged on his chin between draws on the slippery end of his cigar. "Well, it is a good distance from High Valley down to Ruby Valley, Utah, around three-hundred miles as the crow flies. But the price is right. They'll pay five-thousand dollars at one-hundred twenty-five a head for forty of our finest mustangs. They call 'em "native stock" which we pride ourselves in. They've been buying them out of California but since the route is more central to us, it'd be cheaper to buy them from us."

Mary Ellen addressed her immediate question. "Can I go with you Yancy? I know how to drive a herd. How long do you think it'd take?"

"Most likely we could do it in about two weeks one way," he figured.

"What about Ma? Will she put up a fight? I'll do chores ahead and you could talk her into it. Is Jasper and Dash coming along? You know we'll get along just fine, and I've ridden with them to gather the wild ones. What do you say Yancy, take me with ya?"

"Take a breath there Mary Ellen let me figure it all out on paper first. You've got lessons to think about."

"Yeah but, my lessons are on the trail, right? I got a lot to learn and it'd only be for two weeks," she looked into his gray eyes pleading with every facial muscle she could muster up.

"Well, I'll talk to your mother. I could use you as our fourth drover since you know the mustangs, but you'll have to toe the line, you know that don't ya? What I say goes and you'll be obeying my rules, right?"

"Of course Yancy, okay, of course, I won't let you down!"

So the round-up began. Yancy had to choose the best of his lot to be eligible to withstand the grueling race and distance of the Pony Express owner's expectations. The route had been laid out over a distance from St. Joe, Missouri to Sacramento, California. It took some negotiating every inch of it before they started dropping money into stations built every ten or so miles a part. The intent was to be the fastest delivery of mail crossing the country as possible. The railroad wasn't connected yet from east to west, and the telegraph was good in the east, but not completed in the west at least not consistently. So with those gaps and the brewing of war hissing like a massive rattle snake between the States, it was mandatory that the country be linked to each other for important economic and political reasons.

Abe Lincoln was only a couple of months away from getting elected as president of the U.S. which made critical demands on seeing the mail through from coast to coast. William H. Russell, Alexander Majors and William B. Waddell, all pioneer freighters and stagecoach operators took on the business to make the Pony Express work.

They needed about four to five hundred horses over one-hundred stations and a fresh rider every seventy-five to one-hundred miles. This put the Treadwell Mustang Ranch on a special list to provide horses.

The Company plan was to begin the first ride on April 3rd of 1860. The route was divided into three sections, the eastern, from St. Joe to Salt Lake City. This section was already an established stage line, but further westward, the business had to build a new series of stations through mountains, plains, and desert to California. The central line was from Salt Lake City to within the last three-hundred miles of Sacramento.

It was now early July and another forty head were needed to cover the stations from Ruby Valley, to Black Rock, Utah just about twenty-four station rides or two hundred forty miles.

Yancy made a deal with Solomon to drive the horses to Ruby Valley where he would deliver the herd and be paid in full.

It was Dash Lane who seemed to like Mary Ellen the best between him and Jasper Jones. Even though he'd never let her know, but took her under his wing on those rides up into the mountains to hunt Mustangs. Yancy could take his eye off his impetuous granddaughter when Dash was along. Dash was glad when he heard the news about the Pony Express drive that Mary Ellen was coming along.

Jasper, on the other hand was growling about the prospect, just his luck he'd have to deal with Mary Ellen. "Kk-hrist," he spouted, "What's Yancy lettin' her come for? Girls don't belong on a drive like this! She'll just slow us down, probably get hurt. He just cain't say no to that girl!"

"Oh stop your moanin,' Jasper. You sound like your ass is blistered! What could possibly happen on a two week drive that would be Mary Ellen's fault?"

"A hell of a lot Dash, just wait and see!"

"Well stop your belly-achin', she's goin' and if you want your job, you'll just do your job!"

Dash was the older of the two men, in his mid-thirties while Jasper had lived through twenty-seven winters since his birth one frigid November midnight. Dash put up with him, but it wasn't always easy, and Mary Ellen just didn't like him and told Yancy and Dash so.

"One thing you gotta learn in life Mary Ellen is that you're not gonna like everyone, so get used to it Squirt," Yancy spit out a stray tobacco tidbit.

"Don't call me that Yancy; it's not respectful. My name is Mary Ellen!"

"Okay M-a-r-y E-l-l-en," he smiled "...but remember, Jasper's a good wrangler and knows horses. His temperament ain't great, but he can face a quagmire and come out okay. He may save your neck!"

Mary Ellen looked at Yancy square in the eye and said, "Yeah, I know Granddaddy, and I might save his!"

It had taken about six months for the boys to break the mustangs for riding and for what was needed to tune 'em up the Company could do the rest after they arrived at their stations.

The day finally came, after rounding up the herd and making preparations for food, equipment, and the trail they would take to provide enough water and grazing for a fortnight of travel. Each drover was expected to take care of their own horse, tack, belongings and cooking utensils.

"Ye up Brownie," Mary Ellen gave him a good kick, time to go. She'd checked and double checked her gear, her cinch and blanket and turned Brownie toward the pasture that was filled with the forty head of multi-colored bays, palominos, appaloosas, blacks, paints, whites and chestnuts as they sniffed the expectant air. They'd grazed for a few days while the hours collided into day and another night before the opened gate invited them into the fenceless land. Nobody had to coax them to shed their confines, but once the stallions bolted through the gate the mares followed and cantered to catch up.

Jasper rode a red roan gelding named Buster while Dash sat on a horse that was seventeen hands high; her name was Figure Eight. She was a white-faced tri-color paint who commanded respect in any parade. Yancy rode Snort. Snort was getting up in years but was the most experienced horse on the ranch. He was the best example of an American horse, black as night and a wild mustang tamed to ride but still possessing wild instincts that were bred into him from his wild days running free.

The three men and Mary Ellen picked up speed as the pasture emptied, and it was up to them to herd this wild bunch south. They would be riding in desert landscapes and crossing the Snake River before they crossed the northern Nevada border, but first they would take the herd through mountainous, heavily treed terrain. The morning sun burned into noon as the horses slowed to a walk through the forest.

Droving through forested land was slow and took the better part of a day. The four ate in the saddle getting down from their horses long enough to relieve themselves. Riding took tenacity as it sometimes was long and boring and slow. They wanted to get out of the mountains before sunset. They wouldn't bed down until they were out in the open under the stars.

Yancy kept his eye on Mary Ellen for the first ten miles, just making sure that she and Brownie were getting the hang of moving the great body of horses. The herd fell into a moving trance. As long as they were moving they stayed out of trouble. The cracking of downed sticks and branches on the forest floor drowned out the yips, and yaws, and whistlin' hat-slappin' drovers. The last ten miles to camp, Yancy relaxed in the saddle and just forgot about Mary Ellen.

As the shadows grew long, Mary Ellen was feeling a powerful hunger and tiredness as the sun began its descent across the bare land with its rocky soil spreading out from the edge of the forest into what looked like oblivion! She swore she wasn't going to complain, but would pull her weight like she told Yancy she would!

She galloped up to Yancy and before she could ask him, he gave the halt sign that said, Here. We'll park 'em here tonight. There's just enough light to get laid out and set up camp.

Dash built a fire and the four gathered round after they pulled out their beans, hardtack, and biscuits. "Pretty good day," Dash spoke up. "I think Jasper if you'll take the first watch tonight I could relieve you around midnight?" Jasper grunted yes and Yancy said he'd get some shut-eye and take the third watch, around three o'clock. "Mary Ellen, I'll want you to join me on one end of the herd about the same time, better unsaddle and set your bed, it's almost dark."

They finished supper and Jasper left the three others sitting around the fire for a spell more while he turned Buster toward the herd. Mary Ellen was so tired she could barely speak, but mustered up the energy, said goodnight and before her head hit her saddle pillow she was out.

The next thing she knew, Yancy was pulling at her blanket to wake her. She rubbed her eyes, pushed her hair away from her face and sat up. "Okay, Yancy, I'm comin'".
She saddled Brownie who had been sleeping soundly and harrumphed when the bit hit his teeth. She joined Yancy riding a sleepy horse.

It was dark even though the moon cast light upon the land. She asked her granddad what it was like riding in the dark. "I mean I wonder how those Pony Express riders can run all night when they can't see where they're goin', seems impossible!"

Yancy pointed up to the full moon on this first night of August. "Well, the moon helps a lot and when it's dark then the stars will point the way."

"Which stars do you look at Yancy?

"Well, see the Big Dipper there?"

"Yup," as she followed his outstretched arm and down his pointer finger to the Big Dipper, "See Polaris, it's called the North Star. It sits about five fingers from one of the pointer stars on the dipper part of what's called the Plough. If you find that, you'll know where you are. Follow up from the pointer star and you'll always find it." The North Star never changes. See it?"

"Yeah, I see it Yancy."

"So if I look in the opposite direction, it'll be south, and the same with east and west?"

"Well, just remember this, you know what Orion is, look, there it is. You'll see the three stars in a straight line, his belt. Just know that if you're out all night like we are tonight, you watch it as it always rises in the east and sets in the west. You won't get lost Mary Ellen if you know the direction you need to go. Never fear the dark on a starlit night. You'll always find your way."

Mary Ellen stared at the faint form of the constellations as they began fading as first light began to roll across the eastern sky. She was fully awake now, even though Brownie was cocked on three legs like horses do when they sleep standing up. Her watch was over. She rode into camp just as Dash and Jasper were mounting their horses.

"Time to move 'em out," Dash barked. "We got to make at least thirty miles today."

The emptiness of trees and the immersion of clean blue sky and yellow August grasses caught the landscape of the basaltic rocky soil of southwestern Idaho country that early morning. Once the herd began to move, dust rose causing the drovers to pull up their neckerchiefs over their mouths and noses. The summer of 1860 was proving hot and dry.

Mary Ellen wore dungarees that her mother made her especially for the trip. The soft cotton her mother used, she doubled to make stronger to withstand the long hours of riding in the saddle. The pants protected Mary Ellen from sunburn, biting insects, and saddle chafe but, once doubled was hotter than blazes. The sun had just been up an hour before she started to sweat. Thirty miles today, she thought. She pushed the thought from her mind, pulled her felt cowboy hat down over her eyes a ways to keep the blazing sun at bay and flanked the herd whooping and slapping her lariat against her saddle.

By the end of the day, her boots were covered with dust and her face was dirty from where the scarf had been tied. It was like a perfect boundary line between her eyes just to below her chin.

It was the fourth day now and by tomorrow afternoon, they'd be crossing the Snake River as they moved closer to the Pony Express line into northwest Nevada Territory.

Nevada wasn't even a territory yet let alone a State, but would be within a year, and four years. With each mile, the soils became layers of sand, imbedded with silt and sometimes gravel. Canyons sunk deep into the landscape after volcanic waves formed the Owyhee and Snake River Plain. The summer skies showed no sign of storms, but the sun pounded into the earth and the wind was still once they reached the Snake.

This was the territory of the ancient first Americans: Shoshone, Bannock, Northern Paiutes and Paiute Indians. It was a terrible time for Indian tribes all over the Frontier during the 1850's through the '60's and 70's as the Federal Government was destroying their culture and ecosystems to force them to live on reservations that were decided in Treaties across the west through tricks of speed, false pretense, lies, and violence. As much as Yancy was a rancher sitting on a large piece of property once tribal lands, he felt he understood the Indian's dilemma---the flood of "Westward-Ho Progress" wasn't going to be stopped now no matter how much he sympathized.

Dash talked about the trouble the Paiutes had over the last two years after the federal army forced them to leave their tribal lands to reservations. The area was not like the Pacific Northwest Peoples where food and shelter was abundant, but of sparse resources of desert lands where their subsistence counted on deer, rabbit, grasshoppers, rodents, seeds, nuts, berries, and roots. When hoards of Europeans and livestock overtook and trampled the land, the Indians began to starve.

"Most white folks hate 'em, but I figure what choice do the Indians have? The waves of these folks pouring in from the East are affecting everything out here on the Frontier. We ranchers will be next someday, and we'll have to fight to keep our land and our ways, Wish it weren't so." Dash added. "Not much we can do about it though." Mary Ellen was leaning on her saddle horn. "Yancy said he's lookin' to hire a couple of Shoshone to help us take the herd cross the Snake. He's out scoutin' for 'em now."

This was the first time for Yancy to swim a good size herd across the river and he wasn't a hundred percent sure what the best place was to make a safe crossing.

Jasper was with the herd waiting for Yancy to return. The sun was high in the sky; the day was heating up and proving to be a scorcher. There was little shade to find relief so horses and humans just sweltered. Flies were buzzing and landed making themselves at home on sweaty arms, faces, and bare necks. Horse flies were the real enemy. As the horses stood in clusters, Mary Ellen watched as they swished their tails and shivered their necks to be rid of the irritating blood suckers. Yancy better hurry, she thought. This waiting was unbearable! "I think I'm gonna burn up Dash! Where do you think he is?"

Then she saw dust rising in the distance. As the riders got closer, she saw Yancy galloping with two Shoshone toward the herd. It was a sight to behold. The two Indian men rode bareback. They rode with a thin rope, like a hackamore to control their charges. They were dressed in buckskin pants that were made out of deerskin. A breechclout was fashioned around their waists; their hair was half loose with two braids in the front flying in the wind. Hawk feathers clung inside the plaiting and bent under the breeze. One wore a large, crude gingham cotton shirt with two arm bands. Each had choker necklaces handmade out of bone and beads. One was younger than the other so Mary Ellen thought they might be kin, like father and son.

As they rode up, she saw their faces were rugged and browned to a deep bronze. The elder man had deep creases that resembled a cut bank that'd been eroded over years of exposure to sun, rain, and freezing cold. The younger's eyes were penetrating as he surveyed the mustangs, drovers and Mary Ellen. She didn't mean to stare, but couldn't help it, not for a second.

The three men slowed to a trot, then stopped suddenly causing swirls of dust to hug their mount's feet. There were no introductions as Yancy gave the men the lead to show them the way to the river crossing. Mary Ellen was told to ride out to Jasper while Yancy and Dash pushed the herd toward the Indians where they moved out front making way to the great Snake. The herd began to move slowly at first. When the riders whooped 'em up, they struck out following the two Shoshone down a steep hill of rock and sand to end up at the bottom only to take another hill. As they reached the top of the second hill, there was the Snake.

The river looked completely calm as it chugged west, didn't seem at all dangerous to Mary Ellen, but she knew better after listening to the men talk about how many lives were taken every year by a river that appeared tame. Swimming any animal across was a risk. Mostly cattle fall victim to terror if they only had themselves to make decisions. Inevitably, they'd swim half way across then turn back in panic. It became common knowledge that the horses should be swum first to make a wake for the cattle to follow.

Yancy really wasn't sure just how deep the river would be, but it wasn't just the depth that was cause for concern, but the current could get nasty. They didn't want to waste any time getting the horses in the water and pushing them across, the less hesitation the better. The Indians rode up the river until they pointed to the best place to cross. They would help get the herd into the water and swim them through then their job would be done.

"So Yancy, where do you want me," Mary Ellen shouted excitedly.

"You let the lead horses get into the water, and then take Brownie in on the downriver side of the herd. Keep your eyes on the Shoshone as they swim in front of the herd. Brownie will follow them!"

Brownie's nostrils flared as she gave him the go kick. She tied the string on her hat tight under her chin and made noise that Brownie understood. He was on his own in the water. He'd swum before with a natural confidence, but he just didn't have anybody on his back. The herd entered the water, neighing and snorting objections but soon taking the water like mustangs, with force and determination. As the river's flow rose up to their chests, they began to become buoyant and the moment they lost contact with the bottom, they began to swim.

A quarter of the herd was in the water up to their necks. Their bodies drifted in the current as they approached the middle, but they pushed on eyeing the horse in front of them. The Indians humped forward on their mounts breaking the slow chugging current. The whole time they were whooping making an audible wake for the only thing above water: horse heads and ears. What a scene, hawk feathers and black braids wet on gingham, the father and son staying seated until the lighter of the two rolled into the water. The water just loosed him from the back of his horse. He began drifting in the current, but as he floated to the rear of his horse he reached out and grabbed its tail. His horse became the boat as he became the keel.

If water could freeze in the middle of an eighty-five degree summer day it might appear so in the breathing of one single mass of animals, hearts and lungs invisible through the depths of the mighty Snake River—flowing like it always flowed west and north to the mouth of the Columbia in Central Washington Territory which eventually emptied into the Pacific Ocean at "Cape Disappointment." As the Snake embodied all the mustangs and the riders, Mary Ellen found herself, like the young Shoshone floating above her saddle. Her first thought of fear of drowning entered her mind.

There was no crying out for help. Her salvation was at stake however everyone had their own survival at hand and would never have seen, let alone been able to help her. She either found a way, got lucky, or just drowned. As Brownie swam, Mary Ellen found the weight of her water-filled cowboy boots and clothes drag her down into the depths of the green deep current. She struggled only to keep her face out of the water. If it hadn't been for Brownie who stopped swimming to let the current take him toward Mary Ellen she may well have had one more gulp of air before she gave way to the current and slipped away. When she felt him against her, her eyes wide at the surface water, she thrust her hand through a stirrup and held on. Brownie began swimming again in powerful strokes. The force of the water thrust her face above and she took a breath that brought her head all the way up. She tried to kick her feet to help her horse, but was too waterlogged. Brownie's eyes were wild with the threat, but he just kept swimming for the shore.

When Brownie found ground, Mary Ellen let go. Her shoulder hurt as she dragged herself through the remaining three feet of water until she collapsed on the beach of the opposite shore. The herd bucked forward pulling water with them; each mustang shed water like thick moss on a waterfall. Dash and Yancy saw Mary Ellen flounder on the sand, unable to move. "Get er' Dash," Yancy spit it out, "...you're closer." Dash pulled his dripping mare to the girl. "Mary Ellen, can you hear me?" He jumped out of the saddle and found her utterly exhausted but she gave this little signal, groaning with pain, that she was alive. Dash tried to pick her up, but she cried out, "No Dash! It's my arm, don't touch it!"

When Yancy rode up, Jasper was right behind him. Both men got off their mounts and closed in on Mary Ellen. It was Jasper who sized up the situation right away. He'd seen Brownie pull her to shore. "It's your shoulder isn't it girl?"

"It hurts!" she groaned, "Don't touch it Jasper! I think it's broke. Yancy don't let him touch it!" Mary Ellen began crying. The pain was so severe she threw up. "We have to turn you over Mary Ellen," Yancy took control and said, "You must turn over Mary Ellen, come on, I got you." Her granddad gently began moving her onto her back. The other two men helped raise her body up on the grassy shore. There, Yancy examined her shoulder. Mary Ellen screamed.

"I see the problem now. Mary Ellen you've dislocated your shoulder. It's gonna hurt like hell until it gets put back into your socket." Mary Ellen screamed between sobs, "What are you gonna d-o-o-o, Yancy? Don't touch it, n-o-o Granddad," she shrieked! Yancy gave Jasper and Dash the look for them to hold her down. She was thrashing in agony; water was flying into the low-sun leaving light shining over the sand and the men and Mary Ellen. He pulled her arm straight out and gave a jerk. She gave a piercing cry and passed out. Mary Ellen was the only casualty at the river crossing.

Before sundown the men made a bed on soft ground, giving up their own blankets to cushion the girl. Even though it was hot enough to not require a fire they built one anyway. Mary Ellen needed to be kept warm throughout the night. She fell into a deep sleep to shake off the trauma.

As the sky was growing dark, the three sat down together with the Shoshone to make good for their services. The elder man knew some English learned from his doings with whites crossing the river. Between his broken English, Shoshone tongue and sign talk they were able to have a conversation about the day. Yancy told them what they were doing with driving the herd of mustangs to the Ruby Valley Pony Express station.

The Shoshone said that it wasn't a good time. "Too many killings by Paiute brothers against Army, killing many settlers for starving out Indians," he said as he sat on his haunches. "Paiute have enough. You go, you face violence."

Yancy tipped his hat to them in respect, gave them money along with a fist full of buttons and strips of colored ribbon. They took the pay, turned and walked to their horses, mounted and disappeared into the dark.

"Makes me wonder if they'd get caught by the Paiutes what they'd pay if they found out they was helpin' whites cross the river." Jasper winced. "Well, this trip might get dangerous. Better be on the move and keep an eye out round the clock."

In the morning, Mary Ellen was hungry. Yancy told her they'd feed her after he bound up her arm so she couldn't move it. "You're gonna be sore for a spell Mary Ellen, but you're young and it'll heal quicker than you might think. You'll ride at the back of the herd from here on out. You've earned your stripes girl" he winked.

Two days had passed since crossing the Snake and Mary Ellen was feeling better. By the end of the day her shoulder began to ache like a son-of-a-gun, but throughout the day she rode consistently and toughed out Brownie's trots when he foresaw the possibility of some of the herd straying or lagging behind.

Utah Territory was within a day's ride now so it looked like she could see the end of the trail. The pace was steady and ever since the crossing some days ago, she began moving her arm away from her body. She exercised it in the saddle pushing to be free of the confines of injury.

Mary Ellen loped Brownie up to Dash. "Should be one more night out before we get to the station and offload the herd," he said.

Mary Ellen was so excited to actually see a Pony Express Station for real. Maybe she'd get to see a rider come riding in at top speed as the station horseman was there ready with his next mount.

How romantic, she thought. "I can't believe it" she said under her breath.

They were with the herd the last night. The moon was going dark now so the night was spangled with constellations and stars. She found Polaris where true north lay and she found Orion as he rose in the east. She knew the rider would be coming from California tomorrow heading east with his mochila filled with important messages. She could barely sleep with her head full of images of horses, dust, and pounding hooves.

The day began before dawn, right at first light. The drovers would waste no time heading the herd west to Ruby Valley. There was an air of expectancy riding this day. Jasper, Dash, Yancy, and Mary Ellen were aware of time coming to an end when a job was finished. A sense of satisfaction came in the breeze. It was August 13th, the day they'd been riding toward for two weeks.

It was almost ten miles from the Ruby Valley station and all seemed well until about eight of the mustangs spooked and turned south at a gallop. Jasper and Mary Ellen were first to go after them. Jasper signaled with his arm high in the air for her to take the few horses that were galloping off to the east. She split off yee-hawing Brownie as loud as she could. She lost sight of Jasper as he pursued the others veering west.

Mary Ellen was determined to get the mustangs back on track. Nothing was going to delay delivering the horses today! She pushed Brownie to his limit as they gained ground to turn the three. They raced through a small canyon into a wash when she saw him.

There lying face down was a man. He looked small and crumpled, but the most unusual thing was that he was filled with arrows; there were so many. She reined Brownie in hard.

"My God, what is this," she whispered. She rode up to the body and jumped down from the saddle. This "man" was no more than a boy! He couldn't be as old as she was. His blond hair was streaked with blood where an arrow had hit him at the base of his skull. She looked around the site to find a mochila lying thrown into the rocks. His horse was nowhere to be found. "Oh my God," she gasped. As she collected herself it sunk in, that he was a Pony Express rider, "…but he's just a boy" she muttered in shock. In the next moment, fear gripped her that maybe she was next. She ran for rocks to hide herself. She almost stumbled over the body of a Paiute who'd been shot right through the heart. As she slowly began surveying her surroundings she saw another fallen Indian shot twice. How many more were here she gasped?

Jasper came galloping into the wash. "What the hell's taking you so…" when he saw the deadly business, he pulled Buster to a halt. He saw Mary Ellen standing in shock by the two dead Paiutes. "Mary Ellen, get out a here!"

When she spoke her voice commanded Jasper to go get help! "No!" she said. "I will stay with the body until you get help. The Indians are gone now. They must've taken the boy's horse and rode west!"

Jasper, not one to wait, told her he'd be back within the hour.

Mary Ellen waved him off.

The sun was so low in the sky dusk would be coming soon. She picked up the mochila and opened the pockets to see how important the letters were. There was a letter to Tennessee from a John Bell in Sacramento. It had an official seal on it so Mary Ellen thought it must be important. She walked around the battle area only to find five more dead Paiutes. This boy killed seven Indians by himself while he was being shot full of arrows. After counting the arrows in the boy, there were fourteen.

In moments, she vomited on the ground then the craziest thought piled into her brain. The mail must go through! This boy couldn't die in vain!! She knew he was riding east so that was what she needed to do. Egan station was possibly fifteen miles away. I can do that she thought. She took the boy's hat, threw her own on the ground and put his on, grabbed the mochila and threw it over her saddle. She climbed back on Brownie and gave him a kick and headed in the opposite direction of Ruby Valley.

As Brownie picked up speed, Mary Ellen was filled with fear. What if I'm riding toward them? The idea had to be thwarted, she could do it, must do it no matter what the danger is. She was on a mission, the second mission of her life—first to drive a herd across a major river, and almost dying, and now through sheer accident, she comes across the dead Pony Express rider only to take up his stead to deliver the mail on time.

She'd never been on the route so could only ride knowing about the stories that were told to her around the campfire by the men. There's no stopping if you can help it, but you ride strapped for leather! Just ride Mary Ellen! RIDE!

Night was quickly falling. She would have to guide Brownie. As dark moved across the sky from east to west, the stars and constellations grew brighter. She kept up the pace as she sped across the desert landscape. While holding on as tight as she could to the saddle horn and reins, Brownie jumped small gullies finding his footing. She took her eyes off her horse's neck long enough to look up and find Polaris. The great Orion was rising in the east. She thought to just keep Brownie heading toward the belt just like Yancy told her.

Coyotes howled in the void as she held on. She hadn't noticed before, but after riding full out, her shoulder began to hurt. She'd switch hands, one to hold the reins, the other to grip the saddle horn.

As she scanned the distance for Egan station as it must be coming up, finally, her eyes fell on a light ahead. This must be it, she thought. Brownie saw it too and headed straight for it. He was lathering from the all out ride and would welcome a break, but it wasn't to be.

There were men waiting for her as she came careening into the station. She was breathless but before she got off Brownie a station keeper ran up to her and told her they'd been attacked that afternoon by Paiutes on the war path. They were lucky to have enough warning and guns to thwart a wipe-out, but they'd run off the available waiting horses so the Indians couldn't get them. Mary Ellen thought these must've been the Indians who got into the fight with the Pony Express rider. She couldn't stop long enough to tell them the details of what she'd found, but just warned them about the death of the rider. Someone was getting help and she took off in a bolt.

It all took a split second, and in that flash during the dark, the station keepers did not see that the rider was a girl. Of course, Mary Ellen hadn't considered for one minute that only men were allowed to be a Pony Express rider. She knew they hired young riders, even in their advertisement they suggested a rider be an orphan because of the intense danger factors. She brushed the thought from her mind and held on tight. Her thoughts that night raced from staying east toward Orion's rising horizon, to holding on, to thinking about Yancy wondering where the hell she was, and being so worried that after delivering the mustangs and getting paid, spent the night out with the boys searching for her. When they couldn't find the mochila at the site they figured she got the notion in her head to ride the mail to the next station. That'd be just like Mary Ellen. Yancy thought, her mother's right I should've listened to her. That girl is wired for risk as if a dislocated shoulder would stop her. He expected to find her resting at Egan station. When he and Dash and Jasper rode in, they were met with the fact that she and her horse rode out for the next station. "My God that girl!!!" Yancy slapped his hat hard against his thigh. "G-I-R-L?" The station master choked. "Yes GIRL!" Yancy spat. "She's on to Schell Creek station. Let's go boys!"

Brownie was so tired he began tripping. "C'mon boy, you can make it." Mary Ellen knew that Brownie would run himself to death if she demanded it so she slowed down her pace. He was loping in when they reached the Schell Creek station. This time, after thirty miles of riding, someone was there waiting with a fresh horse. She leapt off Brownie, hugged his sweaty neck and yelled at the man that she'd be back to get him! Before he could question her she was in the saddle and galloping out of the station toward Antelope Springs.

Boy, the difference between a rested horse and an exhausted one made such a difference, besides this horse knew the route. The mustang gelding was a warm rippling, breathing machine under her small frame. When he took off she wasn't expecting such power. The bay whinnied as his hooves crashed across the creased canyon floor. Every ten miles, she thought. I'll be riding this horse for ten miles then switch again. The distance disappeared so fast that Antelope Springs popped up before she was ready.

Just like clockwork, a horseman was waiting with a Palomino paint ready for the switch. She grabbed the mochila, threw it over the saddle and was in the stirrup in less than a minute. She was getting the hang of this adventure quickly. As the paint ripped out down the route, she saw Orion slip into the western sky. First light was beginning to appear on the eastern horizon. Mary Ellen was sinking a bit in the saddle as her shoulder was fussing like a newborn baby. She dismissed the pain to feel what the paint could do for her. Really, how wonderful it was to ride so many different mustangs in just a few hours. Who would have thought it could be so thrilling to feel each one's personal identity and temperament. She fell in love with each horse that carried her into the dawn. No one could know what it felt like unless they rode the Pony Express route!

Prairie Gate, 8 Mile, Deep Creek, Canyon, and Willow Springs stations rushed by into mid-morning as she rode and changed horses. Not one of the station masters recognized her as a girl. She acted like a seasoned rider, which could only be a male leaving no suspicion for stopping her, besides the mail had to go through!

Yancy and the boys had ridden all night, but certainly not at the pace Mary Ellen rode. They stopped at 8 Mile to rest their horses for a couple of hours. Little did they know that she was coming into her final station, Boyd. She almost fell out of the saddle when she was met by a young sleepy-eyed man who'd just awakened from a full night's sleep. He seemed invigorated and strong. He tipped his hat as she handed him the mochila. In a split second, he was off to Fish Springs station.

Mary Ellen shakily greeted the station master. He pointed her to the bunk house. There was a hot meal waiting for her, but what Mary Ellen was really interested in was water, and lots of it.

"Hey, slow down there fella," the cook said, "You might not down so much water right now." She took one bite of a biscuit as she carried it to a bunk made ready for her. She didn't even take her hat off, but fell back against the pillow as the biscuit fell out of her hand to the floor. In a moment, she was lost to drowning in sleep. During the day of blazing heat Yancy rode Snort to Boyd's station alone. When he got there he asked the keepers to please take care of his horse. He was looking for a young girl who'd just ridden ten stops on the route.

"No sir," the attendant said. "We ain't seen no girl, but the last rider is in sleeping at the bunkhouse yonder." He pointed to a small building.

"No girl." The attendant shrugged.

Yancy took off for the bunkhouse. When he opened the door he saw his granddaughter lying on the bed, her hat still on, with desert dirt on her face. She didn't move when he found his way to the edge of her bed. He knelt down beside her with tears in his eyes he couldn't stop from flowing while he just shook his head in disbelief. Was he proud or just astonished as to who Mary Ellen could possibly be? Could he have ever really known her if not for this?

She began to stir. When she opened her eyes very slowly she saw her grandfather's face screwed up with emotion. He said through tears, "Hi Mary Ellen." She tried to sit up, but her shoulder gave out. "Don't rush up honey, take it slow. You got the mail through!"

Mary Ellen smiled weakly and fell back to sleep.

THE HAUL & BOX-IT RACE

In memory of the 20th century Western
films and their magnificent actors and horses!

The dust was thick and raised high in the air as riders rode in from the Prickly Pear Ranch. They'd gathered there on this 22nd morning of May to run in the *Haul & Box-it* 10th annual race. Now, there were eight contestants signed up for the dangerous dash through Indian Country in Madera Canyon just outside Tucson, seven cowboys and one cowgirl. Some of you older folks will remember five of the famous cowboy/girl heroes of yore on the "Golden Screen" of the 1940's, '50's and '60's like Jimmy Stewart, Glen Ford, and Barbara Stanwyck. These three were giants in the genre just in case you never heard of 'em. The other two actors were of television fame. Bigger than life was a rugged-faced Richard Boone playing the star role as Paladin in "Have Gun Will Travel"

(1957-1963) and popular B movie actor Rory Calhoun whose role as the Texan in the 1958-1960 series "The Texan" sealed his fate to be picked to ride in the *Haul & Box-it Race.*

The rest of you onlookers born later will know the other three legendary contenders as Clint Eastwood, Viggo Mortensen, and Russell Crowe. How these eight ever got picked for this story is a mystery, but that's the way the Old West works; anything goes because after all the Old West is wild and free and has no rules and if it did, nobody would follow them anyway. Hold onto your hats as these feisty breeds fight each other to the start line.

Here they come! I can make out four horsemen who ride abreast in the lead. I know Jimmy Stewart's spirited strong bay Pie, and Rory Calhoun's horse Domino wearing his magnificent black and white paint coat; third was RH Tecontender, or TJ who was known as Hildago, a horse not to be beaten in a race as Viggo Mortensen found out playing Frank Hopkins in the blockbuster movie "Hidalgo," and the fourth horse, Clint Eastwood's dapple grey, almost white, but pale for sure named R8 or "Rate" taken from Revelations 6:8 "So I looked, and behold, a pale horse. And the name of him who sat on it was Death." That would be Eastwood in "Pale Rider," if you saw it; clearly Clint was death riding a horse.

Suddenly, another group of horsemen overtook them and spewing rapturous clouds of dust galloped at full speed, horse's ears laid back while Stanwyck, whip in hand, riding her Palomino, Misty Girl, shoots out in front followed by Crowe on his staunch and fast bay mare, Honey. Crowe meant to take the lead, but Stanwyck sliced him out. As the two fought for the lead, Ford, riding his favorite movie horse Tenny, and Boone on his famous bay Rafter, caught up as the small horde rode furiously for the starting line.

If I didn't know better, looking from where I stand, I'd say these eight riders and their mounts had already crossed some starting line a few miles back. The START line was always in the same place, ten miles west of Sonoita just over the mountains from Madera Canyon. In ten years the line had never moved for the *Haul & Box-it Race.* Still this group of famous western hombres and one mighty mujer were already hauling tail as an anxious gathering of gamblers, onlookers, and past *Haul and Box-it Race* contenders waited at the start line for the riders to slow to a cantor and trot into the circle of excitement for the beginning of the race.

Sam Elliot (yes, handle-bar mustached actor Sam Elliot) was chosen to fire the shot to start the race. He was perched on a platform built just for the honor. When he saw Misty Girl spewing dust on the other contenders as Stanwyck cracked her whip, he muttered, "What the hell is going on here? Hey, "S-L-O-W-D-O-W-N" he shouted as he held the pistol high in the air. When he realized that not one of those riders or horses had any intention of slowing down, let alone stopping to take their place at the start line, he pulled the trigger.

The shot rang out! The people standing around the starting line stopped talking and stared at the ruthless bunch coming on like a cattle stampede. Elliot fired his Colt single action again, twice, three times and then unloaded the remaining two bullets into the air. The people pushed back from getting run down. Men's hats were blown off their heads and ladies skirts caught wind like air balloons.

That's when famous director Sam Peckinpah, the judge of the race, sized it up that none of them was playing by the rules. "Damn 'em," he yelled into the dust and the rush of rifled air. Of course, no one could hear him for the pounding of hooves; all they could make out was Sam's veins bulging like he had a noose around his neck. Peckinpah threw his hat into the dirt and kicked a rock that flew up into the air and hit my favorite character actor Andy Devine in the head. Andy, grabbing his head, teetered, but was able to keep his balance. As he recovered, he spit out, "Dang it Sam, watcha' gone and done that fir? O-w-w-w-ch!" The crowd gasped loudly in surprise and bewilderment, but face it or not these riders and horses had jumped the start line from a mile or two back. Peckinpah and Elliot were fit to be tied!

Now the *Haul & Box-it Race* had its hard and true rules and no cowboy prior to these fools ever changed or ignored them. So the so-called rules are, run ten miles in a dead haul; at the turnaround spot there's a box canyon; enter the canyon and at the wall turn round somehow, without taking down oncoming riders and mounts, then race back out and back to the finish line! Some say it's just inhumane for horses to negotiate the box canyon at a dead run and many a horse and rider didn't make it back. A box canyon is just that, like a box turned on its side, open at one end, canyon walls on both sides that get narrower and narrower as the entrance pares down to meet a solid wall of rock. It's not only a bottle-neck if too many riders enter at the same time but can be a complete train wreck if they tangle up.

The first of the course was rolling with grassy hills with intermittent yucca and juniper trees, and of course the skies are not cloudy all day…but when it rains it unleashes torrents of quick water that has nowhere to soak in, and there is so much of it that it floods arroyos and gulches carving them deep into the earth like the Colorado River carves the Grand Canyon. "If you're caught in a flash flood you might as well bend over and kiss your ass good-by," warned Russell Crowe, and he wasn't kidding. It's not often, but if one who hasn't witnessed a flash flood, and if they're old enough they'd remember "Rawhide," (1958) that great T.V. western where Clint Eastwood got his real start in Hollywood. Violent thunderstorms ravaged the rocky shallow soil in some of the eight seasons on CBS.

Every horse and rider is neck in neck. After a half mile of sprinting Jimmy pulls Pie back and falls a length behind. The others follow suit as Stewart takes charge. Pie responds like an archer relaxing the pull on the bow for a better shot ahead. Ease 'em up and keep 'em from stressin' was the strategy, or so was the main message. Stanwyck didn't see it that way et'all! When the men pulled back Barbara leaned forward and smacked her crop hard. "YE UP!" she yelled. Now, Gypsy Girl was hind-quartered heavy and under her golden hair her muscles rippled while propelling her forward like a submarine, full throttle. Stanwick's body was lighter than drifting cottonwood seed blowing like snow in June. She was slight, petite, and flexible, most likely had a waist only 20 inches to be sure. She wore black, her standard riding color, unless it was brown leather. This race it was black: vest, boots, riding skirt, and a short-brimmed flat hat secured under her chin for a windy advance. Her platinum curls were tight against her face and neck.

Stanwick strategy; she wanted a quarter mile gain if she could get it so wasted no time to lag or follow the boy's lead. She wasn't much prone to that anyway. Now you might know this but a full-grown horse has an eight pound heart! In case you didn't, yes, they are large animals, but the thing about a horse is they've got natural horsepower, which is referred to under any car hood, however mechanically it isn't torque but was first realized by a gentleman by the name of Watt (the same gent who did all that neat stuff with steam engines) made some observations, and concluded that the average horse of the time could lift a 550 pound weight one foot in one second, thereby performing work at the rate of 550 foot pounds per second, or 33,000 foot pounds per minute, for an eight hour shift, more or less. He then published those observations and stated that 33,000 foot pounds per minute of work was equivalent to the power of one horse, or, one horsepower. Interesting isn't it? It's the torque that gives the horse-back rider and the car driver the sensation of power surge. Just think that any given car, in any given gear, will accelerate at a rate that exactly matches its torque curve (allowing for increased air and rolling resistance as speeds climb); this same torque propels the horse by increased air through the lungs. Torque rules at the starting line, but the heart determines endurance and stamina. It is true that a horse possess' the power to run itself to death for its rider. They have the "heart" to sacrifice on command, not like a mule which thinks first and rarely agrees. You see, horses have a special heart, like some humans. This is why we say someone has heart!

Barbara knew Misty Girl had torque, horsepower, and heart the same way every rider racing in the *Haul and Box-it Race* knew what their steed was capable of, however, this race was one of strategy and partnership, not just to win for personal ego, or so we think. Whatever the winning prize it didn't seem to matter to these start-line deviants! So what was their motivation?

A half hour had gone by since the eight had tricked the onlookers at the starting gate. Peckinpah and Elliot were heatedly discussing disqualifying the whole bunch and were dead serious about doing it. Matter-of-fact, they would disqualify them, dagnabit! And who in God's name would've thought Jimmy Stewart would do such a thing anyway? So, according to the two rule-keepers these cowboys were just racin' for the fun of it! They threatened the prize money was goin' to the sheriff's discretionary fund to keep outlaws off the streets of town, and after the shenanigans of this bunch all eight were considered outlaws, and they might as well keep runnin' up to "Hole in the Wall" hideout in the Big Horn Mountains way up in Wyoming or they'd find themselves in jail!

The early morning sun broke across the canyon bringing with it the promise of another blistering day. Each mile laid behind, beat the increasing heat. The runners were settling in on five miles out with Misty Girl in the lead and Pie thundering behind. Jimmy Stewart was no stranger to westerns or to ridin'. After WWII, where he proved himself as a combat pilot flying behind German lines for twenty sorties, he started making westerns and knocked off, *Broken Arrow* (1950), *Winchester '73* (1950), *Bend of the River* (1952), *The Naked Spur* (1953), *The Far Country (1954)*, *The Man from Laramie* (1955), *Cheyenne Autumn* (1962), and *How the West Was Won* (1964) to name a few. He was tall and lean and was envied for his natural acting voice. He never played a bad guy but was known for his portrayals of diffident but resolute characters.

Russell Crowe knew who he was up against. He'd had some big roles in movie making too such as Roman General Maximus Decimus Meridius in *Gladiator* and bad guy Ben Wade in *3:10 to Yuma*, his one well known western. If anyone could carry off competing with this group of sage riders, it was Crowe. He decided to make Honey a contender leaning into the hoof-kicked dust he je-hawed and let her have her head. Crowe sat heavy and settled in the saddle, his muscular thighs executing squeeze-power to Honey's torque. He dashed forward leaving the others to make their own decisions. He didn't look back, but fixed his narrowed green eyes on the distant rugged rocks. The box canyon couldn't be much more than four miles away. He'd work Honey another mile for sure then begin negotiating his approach and positioning his entry.

Viggo is a horseman. You can tell by his posture when he rides. His seat is as straight as a masthead as he presses his knees ever so gently into TJ's ribs. The fine-tuned rider and horse have powers together, both mastering them one to the other. Viggo taps, TJ responds. They rode forth with mesquite blurring under belly and hoof. Viggo continued his trajectory, picking up speed, staying clear of flying dust and debris. He figured he had a desert to spread out; when it was time to thread the needle he'd have it well thought out.

Boone was the heaviest in the saddle, now middle-aged and thick, his facial features resembled drought in mud. He was no pretty boy and knew it.

He was an actor more than a rider and could scare the crap out of anybody if he wasn't on his side. Richard was a bit of a dichotomy—he looked so mean, but he played the white hat in his TV show. He was his own man, frightening to the bad guys and seriously appreciated by the good 'uns (you could see he was good natured especially when he tipped his hat back on his head and leaned on the saddle horn real friendly like), but more than that, he was a warrior. The paladins, sometimes known as the Twelve Peers, were the foremost warriors of Charlemagne's French court; pretty nifty on the part of CBS, to give him the name of Paladin, huh? Paladin was a fast draw, but like a cat enjoyed the foreplay before he pulled the trigger on his Smith & Wesson handgun and brought his adversary to dirt. He was like a Rottweiler when he set his mind and here no different was gripping the reins while floating in the saddle from side to side in full gallop. Rafter was used to his clumsiness, but forgave him because he had heart, and he was big enough to handle Boone. He wasn't hot-blooded like an Arabian or Thoroughbred, but what they call cold-blooded, beings that he was part Quarter horse and Percheron which cut him back on speed, but his endurance and stamina most likely gave him a ten pound heart. He could crash into the walls of the box canyon and take it in stride.

Eastwood really didn't like to run full out. He usually loped. He didn't have to be fast because he was never running away. He was going to and usually found a slow deliberate entrance into enemy territory. Why sneak when you're so merciless? No terrible, horrible, murderous, snake-eyed, liquored-up, filthy, stinkin,' rotten,' rapin,' scum could possibly take him, 'cuz he was worse. Rate was a perfect foil for Clint. The mare was calm, almost lackadaisical, essentially unmotivated, and could nap at any given moment. Rate had no interest in racing preferring the gentle canter that Eastwood controlled. So how did they end up in the *Haul and Box-it Race*? Suspicion says to intimidate the others by just showing up at the Prickly Pear and got caught up in the moment. Whatever reason would there be? They moved off to the east.

Calhoun and Domino watched Rate move away from the others. Little did he suspect that in the middle of a race, Eastwood would just keep heading east until he was-- gone? He didn't give it any more thought as he was only a few fractions behind Boone. Domino had suffered a bruised hoof a few weeks back so treated tender might keep him from getting lame today. Ride easy not ruthless like Stanwyck running poor ole Misty Girl just for a gain before the box canyon. As much as Rory was a lady's man, with his white straight-toothed smile which lit up his pale turquoise eyes and that little dimple (or is it a scar) just under his left eye where the cheek scrunches up, he never did take much to Barbara. He preferred a bosom with a lift and buttocks that looked big in a bustle. Barbara was too pushy and boyish, in spite of her fight for women in Hollywood to be the boss, matriarch, and ranch owner. He preferred his blondes to need protection, which of course he rescued regularly in movies and his TV series. Calhoun was born Francis Timothy McCown until his name was changed by Henry Willson to Rory Calhoun, a perfect name for an Irish bad boy beauty. It wasn't all movie hype either, because before Calhoun was twenty-one he had stolen a revolver at thirteen and was sent to the California Youth Authority's Preston School of

Industry reformatory at Ione, California. He escaped from the "adjustment center" which was an internal jail within a jail then recaptured for robbing several jewelry stores and a car he drove across state lines (a federal crime). He was sentenced to three years in the penitentiary at Springfield, Missouri. He wasn't released, but was transferred to San Quentin for other offences after he served his sentence. I'd say his first twenty years were rough, but after twenty-one, he got lucky! After seven years incarcerated, what are the chances of being discovered for the movies?

The front runners began to let up as the running was getting to the turn. Nostrils flared bright pink and as Stewart rode up next to Misty Girl Stanwyck knew she had to quit pushing. She dropped to a lope which rendered Jimmy a slight lead before he too pulled Pie in. Glenn had thought about cashing in the race about a mile back. After all, there were no cameras rolling and he had a date with Rita Hayworth, and he wasn't getting paid! He'd been galloping along in a steady fashion to show a good face while the whole time Tenny was giving heart. Would he even make the canyon, and if he did had he a plan?

Glenn made many movies in his day and the best western in my view was *Cimarron* (1960). The Great Land Rush scene in Oklahoma seized my psyche and made its blaze for life. Somewhere in my genetic western coding Yancy and Sabra Cravat, played by Ford and Maria Schell never aged but were indelibly freeze-framed in mid-chaos of buckboards, wagons, and frightened horses spurred by farmers, gamblers, immigrants, family men, bankers and about any other man or woman who could ride. They rode like bats from hell disregarding terrain: draws, creeks, rocks, or obstacles like the scattered remains of a covered wagon wrecked in their path, household debris scattered far and wide.

Ford was cute. He, like Rory Calhoun had black wavy hair and striking blue eyes. He was a true lady's man and if at all possible, he'd find romance with leading ladies, Maria Schell included. So it goes the romance was dandy until *Cimarron* was almost completed and when it was they parted unfriendly. Maybe this was why the movie lost money in the end.

i

Stanwyck was impatient. She had stopped to check Misty Girl's cinch. But now she hooked her foot in the stirrup and before she was even in the saddle, she used her crop on her mare's rump. Misty Girl reared back, her eyes excited and wide as she leapt forward as if the movable barrier at the Kentucky Derby starting gate had just sprung open. When Barbara said move, she meant now! She was a nice lady in real life (at least in interviews), but in movies, she didn't hold back when it came to men and horses. She was all about business-her business and it wasn't beyond her to whip some cow-hand thinking he knew how to do something better than she. Woe to him who disobeyed orders. On occasion she'd raise her hand to her lover who inevitably caught her forearm as she raised it above her head to let him have it. This scene was usually depicted on the movie poster to get you worked up over how great this film would be. And this was in the 1950's remember; she wasn't well liked and seemed ominous and a complete bitch but I suspect rumblings of the 1970's Women's Movement were beginning to bubble like steaming mud in

Yellowstone Park's mud pots. Her time had come and she was making a lot of money.

As Misty Girl bolted ahead, it was hard to know what Stanwyck's strategy was to get through the box canyon. It was a half mile ahead which Misty Girl would make short work of in a matter of minutes. Now that Eastwood had ridden out of the race, the number of riders was seven. Viggo was letting TJ have his head as he was out in front finding his own pace. Both horse and rider looked unbothered by the threat riding up quickly behind them. Mortensen was a man that rarely looked back. He was in his own head not feeling the need to check his base. He seemed to mind his own business and a grueling horse race was to be enacted in perfect dignity and trust whether he won or lost.

It was Stewart that surprised everyone. Jimmy usually was a pretty level-headed guy; his attitude about racing was not unlike Viggo's--he wanted to win, but if it meant harming Pie he'd back off, but would he today? At this moment with the box-canyon just ahead, he spurred (figurative because he didn't wear spurs) Pie into a sprint that would wind any beast! He split ahead past Stanwyck who was using her crop with precision, in figure 8 gestures on Misty Girl's sore rump. As he pitched past her he yelled, "GET OVER STANNY, I'M COMIN' THROUGH!"

The others were quickly approaching like a posse riding hard. Ford wasn't having any of this crap about someone else making it to the box canyon first. He leaned as far forward as he could in the saddle and held the reins almost over Tenny's head, just at his ears. The whole time he was yipping and yapping and making a terrible racket, like he was gonna scare the speed out of everybody. Glen was a hell of a rider and was known for it. What he learned from Will Rogers when he was a young lad riding horses on Will's ranch really taught him what he needed to know for making western movies. It was now that he struck his mark.

There it was the opening in the mountain. He could see it plainly now from his distance of five-hundred yards. He'd never thought of it before, but that opening actually got him real excited, as if he was about to enter the woman of his dreams, and we all know who that was; it was Rita Hayworth his red-haired passion that seduced him in *The Redhead and the Cowboy* that now took over his senses and sexually aroused him into box-canyon frenzy. He was stretched out a league ahead of Stewart and Stanwyck and Mortensen. Crowe was pushing Honey into position to overtake Boone and Calhoun. As much as Boone was the biggest man on mount, he could kick harder giving it to Rafter to push his endurance up a notch—speed wasn't exactly Rafter's forte, I mean he was pretty fast, but when tracking, and then sighting the bad guys, he could close in like sparrows after a hawk. Boone, on Rafter evened the odds when Paladin caught up with 'em and it usually wasn't pretty. Somebody who tried to resist got shot! Crowe pushed forward; Rafter pulled out the plug, his hooves hitting the hard pan causing any close-by scorpions or lizards to wonder what the hell just happened as they tumbled a few feet across the sand—that's what we western types know as "hell bent for leather!"

"Here she comes," yelled Rory as he pointed to the box-canyon. Russell heard Calhoun's announcement over the pounding hooves and immediately thought it was time to thread the needle; he pulled his hat down tight on his head and yelled into Honey's ear, "You can do it girl!" Now, that everyone was almost on the box-canyon any strategy just went flying out of their heads. It was going to be a free-for-all that was duly apparent so now it was left up to skill, the ability to stay seated and a lot of lady luck!! Calhoun pushed Domino to his edge and charged forward.

Ford hit the opening first, riding hard into the wide mouth of the canyon. I would have had a box seat at the Opera if I watched from the top of the canyon wall as these crazies rode "hell bent for leather," reins in one hand and the horn buckle in the other. Hats were loosening on heads as mounts sensed what was coming showing the whites of their eyes. Nostrils flared red with each plundered breath—the leather saddles flapped when stirrups fought to be free. This was no time to lose a foot in the stirrup because that'd be the end of it. Once a rein drops or a foot slides out of a stirrup you've all ready lost control and are whirling into some kind of unforeseen destruction.

Stanwyck flies through the canyon entrance next. Her aggression has not subsided one bit. She not only whips Misty Girl, but whips TJ which pisses off Viggo so bad he gives her the finger in mid-sprint. She pays no mind, not for a second but continues her relentless pursuit of Ford. Jimmy is more cautious now. He lets Pie get his grounding even though Pie is agitated by the close quarters. He never did like Misty Girl for whatever reasons and thought to take a bite out of her rump if she dared to bump into him or even come into his line of vision. Stewart was thinking of Pie, as he usually did and reining him in was like downshifting an eighteen wheeler. Jimmy was thinking strategy now, or never! He'd just have to live with whatever happened as he saw the walls of the canyon squeezing in. There was no quitting now! The river was headed over the falls with a current strong enough to move a house; a few horses and riders were nothing to a current like that.

Then, it was a blur. Everyone was in sight of the wall at the end of the canyon. All the horses began to shout in loud guttural voices and for a moment they teetered on the edge of their doom. Honey started bucking as did Misty Girl and Rafter. Hats were flying in all directions and it looked like the calamitous hour of Armageddon!

Glen was out front at top speed when he came face-to-face with the wall. It just came up like a trap door. He pulled back on the reins as if they were train brakes, but to no avail. Tenny rode full steam into the wall with his rider close behind him. The throwing of rock and dirt settled as they both succumbed into unconsciousness, Ford lying in rubble next to the best horse he ever knew made the narrator watch and gasp and cry out. Rory couldn't control Domino now. Domino locked onto Tenny's charge and followed him as he collided with the wall causing him to plow into Tenny's rear-end like he was a tightly coupled train car. Rory flew over Domino's head as his horse buckled to his knees and fell over on his side. Calhoun landed in a sprawl on the ground next to Glenn, the breath knocked completely out of him. When Rory came to and saw the predicament, he desperately tried to navigate away from the other riders on his hands and knees; Boone and Russell were thrown to the ground and Barbara slipped dangerously over the side of Misty Girl but one leg kept her from falling off. Honey lost all sense of propriety and continued bucking wildly before she saw her escape and after rearing in full "Lone Ranger, Silver" style left her beloved Russell to fend for himself on the canyon floor. Rafter was scared off and Domino managed to get back on his feet. His knees were scrapped and torn with bloody rivulets running down to his hocks. Rory wouldn't be riding Domino another step. His race was through.

Richard Boone was cussing and swearing and cursing Stanwyck for being so aggressive (he didn't cite Ford though). Both he and Russell got up like boxers in a ring: ducking and flinching out of the way of horse flesh and sharp hooves. In came Viggo. He sized up the problem reining TJ to the left of the crisis missing the fallen riders and their horses. Once he got around everyone, he moved out of harm's way. Stewart rode Pie in at a trot and yelled into the mayhem, "Is Glenn okay?" Didn't look like Glenn was okay nor was Tenny. Barbara had, with great effort, pulled herself up from her dangling position and reseated herself. Once she made an assessment (Crowe, Calhoun, Boone and Ford were either out of the race or slowed way down). She let out a whoop, turned Misty Girl 180 degrees and started out of the canyon kicking her mount in time with her whip. "My God that woman is a rattlesnake," snorted Mortensen and he pulled TJ around. He told Jimmy he was not going to let Stanwyck win this thing, but before he could get to a full gallop that who should canter in but Eastwood!

"Where the heck have you been?" Stewart demanded.

"To get Midnight," Clint said matter-of-factly.

"Well you could'a let somebody know, it would'a been decent of ya."

"Don't give me any hassle Jimmy. I did what I had to." Eastwood chewed on his cigar stub. "Pale Rider was on her period and wasn't going to give me anything so I went and got Midnight. He wouldn't let me down." Midnight was Rowdy Yate's grand cattle Quarter horse he rode in "Rawhide," and it's true, he never let Rowdy down, not once even in that one episode when a rolling lightening storm started a stampede after blue electricity moved like snakes on Medusa's head across the heads and horns of the cattle.

"Well somebody has to go after Barbara, so you and Viggo get goin'!" Jimmy shouted.

Boone offered, "I'll take care of Glenn and the rest of you should blaze off." He brushed himself off and pulled out his cell phone (which was luckily a satellite phone) and called for a medic helicopter. Once Honey calmed down and came to her senses she galloped back to find Crowe. This was the cue for Russell to get back in the saddle and get back in the race.

Boone shouted, "As soon as I take care of Glenn, I'll be ridin' like Rooster Cogburn in *True Grit* across the field with reins in my teeth so g'wan, git outta here, somebody's gotta win this damn race!" He impatiently waved them away like only a big man can do. Stewart pulled Pie around. Russell was all ready in full gallop making his way out of the box canyon and Mortensen and Eastwood were trailing the little lady who was abusing Misty Girl for her whipping. In just a few minutes they were all clear of the canyon and in full sprint toward the finish line.

ii.

It should be mentioned here that the playing field is leveled between the five remaining riders because all are riding American Quarter Horses! Now this short distance runner wasn't made overnight but was first bred by mixing the blood of a North African Moorish horse with Spanish stock. When the Moors were driven out of southern Spain in the 8th Century the new improved model, better known as the Spanish Barb were brought to the Americas by Spanish conquistadors like Hernando Cortez Pizarro who couldn't have conquered Montezuma and the Aztec/Mexican civilization without them and Francisco Vasquez de Coronado who rode in search of the cities of gold in the American Southwest. When the Chickasaw Indians got a hold of them they fine-tuned them into a more powerful running machine. The colonialists, who loved racing their English horses, began trading with the Chickasaw to improve their stock. Over the next 150 years, the American Quarter Horse became the powerful runner that it is, defined by its ability to reach speeds of 55 miles per hour over a quarter-mile distance, which is why they're called Quarter Horses. If you've never witnessed a Quarter Horse in a barrel race or a calf-roping event at a rodeo it's high time you did! You just can't believe how they dig in and get up to speed in seconds! These majestic creatures canter, or lope along at twelve to fifteen miles per hour, gallop at twenty-five to forty and as mentioned, can reach fifty-five miles per hour in a dead sprint over a short distance like a quarter mile. It's hard to think how fast Glenn and Rory were going when Tenny hit the wall, but I'll bet it was close to 40 miles an hour!

Now, back to the race, Barbara was still leading the pack after a quarter mile out of the canyon. Misty Girl naturally wanted to hold back as she was winded and had no time to process what she'd just been through in the box-canyon. Stanwyck wanted to win the race so bad (these men were mere mortals compared to her goddess stature) and she was sick and tired of having to fight for the roles she wanted as the "boss woman" in her western movies. She signed with Columbia Pictures and at one time was the highest paid woman in America! She was directed by the greats: Cecil B. DeMille, Fritz Lang, and Frank Capa. There was absolutely nothing about Barbara that she was not determined about; she won over all of Hollywood as one of the most prized actresses. An aside says that there were rumors of her being a lesbian, or at least bi which would seem right—she had to be determined!

Misty Girl was breathing heavily. Barbara looked back to see how far out front she was from the others and once satisfied let her horse slow down to a fast canter. It was then that she took her eyes off the terrain ahead and caught a glimpse of the sky. What had been a perfectly clear late dry summer clear-as-a-bell morning was being interrupted by a mammoth cumulus cloud that reminded her of a thunderstorm cell that could build into a dangerous storm.

"What the heck," she thought then muttered, "It's not supposed to rain for another week at least."

Viggo, Russell, Jimmy, and Clint had pulled their mounts back and were loping along together about three-hundred yards behind Barbara. Jimmy caught sight of the now emerging thunderhead and pointed up to the sky. The others looked up and saw the giant darkening cloud that hung just above them. It had a hole big enough for four jetliners to pass through, but you can't find a pilot that's going to fly right through a thunderhead! I can only imagine what was going on inside that thunderhead!

"Well dangit" thought Crowe we weren't supposed to have rain today, not for at least a week! Damn forecasters, they never get it right!" The four horsemen picked up their pace thinking if it began to rain they might be able to outrun it. Now this country is known during the season of wet summer (from July thru September) as monsoon summer. The mornings start out warm and clear but as the heat of the day builds, huge clouds build with it and they're not the kind of clouds that appear black and menacing over a range of mountains, but just like that they appear directly above you like an enormous hovering flying saucer. The upsweep of heated air fills them like a hot-air balloon as they grow into monsters that are sent to devour you if you're out in the open or caught in a canyon, arroyo, or gully.

With a little over six miles left to cross the finish line, the riders decided to run at three-quarter-full-speed-ahead as long as they could. Stanwyck was thinking the same thing as she kicked Misty Girl into action. The grassy, mesquite-dotted flats would reach Little Box Canyon Creek about two miles ahead before the terrain turns toward the trees. They needed to cross before pushing into lower elevations to get to the finish line.

The nervous riders pushed their mounts with more urgency as they race to cross the dry wash before it starts raining. That's just what they need is an Arizona flash flood to contend with. It's been tough enough losing Ford to such a dastardly end in the box-canyon! Running like scared rabbits, it's Stewart who feels the first raindrop. He grimaces and begins to use his reins to whip Pie to take this seriously. Even though Crowe, Eastwood and Mortensen are only a short league behind the rain begins to hit them like a sprinkling of confetti; within two more strides, it's a full downpour. Stanwyck is further ahead, but can she reach the creek in enough time to beat sudden high water? She's riding through the oncoming deluge still pushing for speed, but as the rains go from decrescendo to a pelting crescendo Misty Girl slips on the wet terrain. She doesn't fall, but startles Barbara so she pulls her back to a trot. The others are gaining until they too are forced to slow down in the deafening cloud burst.

Stanwyck can hear Russell shouting above the din, "How much further to the crick?"

"It's about another eighth mile yells Viggo. "I think we'd best get off and walk, maybe that will give us enough time for the storm to pass over."

Jimmy thinks it's a good idea and dismounts Pie. All of them look like drowned rats right about now with small flash floods rushing off the rims of their hats. Barbara isn't convinced that she wants to get down and walk and remember she's closer to the creek than the others. Out of the pouring rain, she eyes the creek just ahead about one-hundred feet. She thinks she can get across before it fills up to make it impassable.

Clint sees the situation as Stanwyck isn't dismounting and continued to push Misty Girl to a fast walk. His soaked cigar stub is dripping and his eyes narrow as he expresses in a low growl, "I tell ya, she's going to be in trouble boys, and we're gonna have to be ready to save her ass."

"I suppose," Stewart replies "…but we oughta let her get into it a little more. We better mount up though."

The five of them begrudgingly remount and start picking up the pace to shorten the distance. Viggo's all ready getting his rope off his saddle anticipating what could happen if the little Box Canyon Creek decided to flash flood—which of course it did just that.

Barbara is almost to the crossing when the water comes slamming down the creek like a tsunami reaching a foreign shore. She tries to turn Misty Girl around, but the muddy rapids catch the horse at her hocks. In just a matter of breaths her feet go out from under her and she's down neighing and screaming in fear. Stanwyck cries out for help as the torrents rush against her. She's got one leg trapped under Misty Girl and can't fend for herself. The horse is gulping in water and trying desperately to get up on her feet, but the water just grows pushing her into a slide.

Barbara screams for help! The four men clamor across slippery rocks until they are dangerously close to being pulled into the swollen creek. Mortensen shouts at Stanwyck telling her that he's gonna throw her a rope. He coils the rope making a lariat; he tries with precision to fight against the distraction of the sheeting rain and judges the throw needed to reach the fallen woman. Clint, Jimmy, and Russell have their ropes ready in case Viggo misses. The whole time Misty Girl's body is holding back water that is rushing to break free over her and spill onto Barbara. She is getting a face-full gulping in too much as she panics in exhaustion. Viggo has to throw because it could be over in just minutes. "HERE COMES THE ROPE, GRAB IT!!"

All the other men start swinging their ropes above their heads making ready to hurl one after another if Viggo and Barbara miss it. Viggo lets go of the rope and it soars against the rain landing on Misty Girl. Crowe and Eastwood let go of their ropes while Jimmy stands back for final back-up. Barbara's face is mostly underwater now and all seems lost until Misty Girl tries one more time to move away from the current. This one act pops Stanwyck up out of the water long enough for her to free her leg. She sees one of the ropes that are laced across her horse and herself and grabs it. It belongs to Mortensen. He quickly pulls TJ into cow-cutting mode and begins to back up dragging Barbara out of the main current. At this point, without Barbara blocking the way for Misty Girl to get any footing, she struggles to claw her way to the edge of the flooding creek. She's huffing and puffing and is genuinely thinking what her next move is. All the cowboys are yelling encouragements to her and Stewart even takes Pie dangerously close to show Misty Girl some solidarity. With one last thrust, she gives it all she's got and works herself to her knees, then in one push, she gets her feet under her and stands up!

"Whoop, whoop" yell the saviors while Barbara is throwing up water and silt from her stomach.

As they all wait in a huddle, a sunbeam breaks from the watery heavens and the rain begins to lessen as the storm moves down the canyon.

Barbara kept saying over and over again, "Thank you boys; thank you; I wouldn't 'av made it if you'd been a moment later." When her breathing became regulated again, she started to get up but the leg that'd been trapped under Misty Girl gave out and she sat down hard.

"Now just take yer time there Barbara. You've had a shave on a blister," Jimmy spoke sympathetically. "There's no need to hurry yourself, or Misty Girl quite yet."

"Thanks Jimmy." She began to untie her kerchief from her slender neck. Once she undid the knot it pulled easily into her hands. She began wringing it out and opened it up for a quick dry. The sun was back out and the heat of the day reclaimed the riders and horses.

Now, the other racers could've left Stanwyck there on the rocks to fend by her self; she'd been beaten soundly, but these cowboys respected her in spite of her obnoxious striving and wouldn't think to leave another "man" down after a harrowing near-death experience. After a few minutes, Jimmy spoke leaning on his saddle horn with his hat tipped back on his head. He rolled his tongue into his cheek and looked down at Stanwyck, "You ready Stanny?"

Viggo, Clint, and Russell had wound up their ropes and were making ready to slowly get the race back into gear. They turned their horses south away from the trees making their way across Little Box Canyon Creek that had slowed to a fast manageable ripple.

Barbara got her footing and limped to her horse. Strangely, Misty Girl seemed eager to run off some pent up energy that had pooled in her veins when her endorphins exploded in the flash flood. She was shuffling nervously when Barbara pulled the reins to the side of the saddle and grabbed the horn to swing up. "Stand still girl!" She commanded. She secured her hat and kicked Misty Girl in the ribs.

She was back in the race.

The third-week-in-June sun usually climbs to around ninety-nine degrees by solar noon – 12:20 p.m. The race began early, just after sun-up and was expected to be finished before the temperatures soared. Horses just aren't built for exertion in extreme heat and if you ever go to New Orleans in May you won't find horses pulling tourists around in buggies in the French Quarter, but you will find mules. They usually wear hats too.

The plan for the *Haul and Box-it Race* was to start at six o'clock and end by noon. Maybe it had to do with the way this particular race began with all competitors not stopping at the start line that made it the most unusual and star-crossed of races yet.

All five riders had bonded due to the flash flood and weren't quite acting out like respectable self-reliant and independent westerners but more like a single-minded clan that had an oath to protect, support, uphold and cover the other—their Creed of solidarity may no longer allow anyone to overtake the other and fight to the finish line.

iii

As the five rode on, they were loping across a stretch of flat grassy land. Their speed was even as they rode like a posse without purpose. It was during this stretch that they noticed they were being passed up on both sides by beat-up half ton trucks, mini vans, motor-homes, and motorcycles. What in blue blazes was going on?

They watched them closely when Clint noticed and said, "Hey these guys are all Indians. What the heck is going on?"

Then riders on horseback racing at full galloped into the mix. Some rode bareback and used hackamores while others looked like they'd had time to saddle up properly. Long black hair was flying in the hot wind and some had eagle feathers tied into thick midnight braids. If Russell didn't know better he'd say these Indians were in some kind of high speed chase. It still wasn't clear whether they were being chased or doing the chasing, but as they overran the racers, they made an awful racket---they were definitely in pursuit.

Dust was kicked up so high that off on the finish line, even with a telescope or binoculars not one thing, horse, man, or vehicle could be made out. Jimmy pulled Pie back to find a place to tie his handkerchief over his mouth. Was this some kind of reenactment or Indian holiday?

Then an Indian riding bareback pulled up on his spotted stallion, dogging Stewart. The two of 'em eyed the other when Jimmy decided to slow Pie almost to a slow lope. He yelled at the guy. "You guys up-in-arms?"

The Indian scoffed, "…you not watch'n the news lately?"

"No, I'm not. I'm racing in the *Haul and Box-it Race* and you guys seem to be in it too. The man told him that his tribe was on the warpath chasing protesters off the reservation. Outsiders wanted to shut their casino down and had blocked roads in and out on the Rez. The Tribal Police were trying to maintain law and order, but they were outnumbered.

They'd had enough of those far-right leaner Christians who knew nothing about Indians but took issue with gambling (it was corrupting good white Christian people). The enemy was using talk radio and T.V. news stories, tweeting and Facebook to get people worked up over the Indian Casinos. They wanted to shut them all down as their God didn't condone gambling and smoking, but deep down the underlying seething was due to so many whites making the tribes rich with their "hard-earned" cash. So it was the Indian's fault that white people gamble and smoke and don't listen to the Lord? These Rance Limburger-Elmer Gantry types know just how to appeal to the far-right masses. Their actions came straight out of a hyped-up Gospel Revival when Tobias Pennywhistle started prophesying straight from God to gather the legions and go down to Arizona, down to the southeastern Madera Canyon country. Old Tobias was weaving back and forth by the time he got the full message— he was thanking and praising God as he shouted out the Old Testament-esk command to go down and block every road in and out of the Rez in Madera Country. When the plan was laid on the holy "Situation Table" in God's "Situation Room" down in Atlanta, Georgia, Limburger took the call and broadcast it far and wide just like a yellow-belly, no good Indian hater.

Jimmy whistled long and loud. Pie wanted to take off, but Jimmy held him tethered. He went on, "What gets into these folks that they think they have the law on their side? Or me'be there's no law at all and just because people have a difference of opinion they can just cause muckraking in someone else's backyard; reminds me of ole Lee Marvin playin' Liberty Valance in *Who Shot Liberty Valance* (1962). I played the hero—Ransom Stoddard—a man of law and order, and no guns!

Marvin was the meanest, shiftiest, murderin' ego maniac Liberty Valance that was ever acted, just like it was written, and it was a woman who wrote the story! Hard to imagine, but I got a lot of respect for Dorothy M. Johnson from out a Montana." Jimmy shifted in the saddle and continued, "...and Burt Lancaster who played Elmer Gantry sure could preach, but he was a terrible sinner according to his own code. Never seems to fail, huh?"

"So this here Limburger fella is supporting the wrong side?" Stewart put together. "Well, I'm sorry to hear it; makes me wonder if he ever saw *Broken Arrow*. That was filmed right here in Apache land. Well, I gotta take off now and get back in the race. Good luck! Hope you push 'em off the Rez, those side-winders," and he knee-squeezed Pie and shouted, "HAW," and Pie dug in like the Quarter horse he was, making short work of catching up with the rest of the racers. As Pie and Stewart galloped full throttle across the valley floor, he could see the spotted stallion kicking up dust as he followed the trail of warriors west until they disappeared along the horizon. When he caught up to the other riders, he confirmed that the Indians were on the war path and for a dang good reason too.

Now that there were only a couple of miles left in the race, the narrator knew what they were all thinking. What else can possibly happen in this race that hasn't happened already? Stanwyck had regained her wild streak and was pushing for the lead, layin' crop on rump. She had that determined look again and it was obvious that to her, the flash flood never happened. Seeing Barbara whip Misty Girl into submission just got Viggo's craw agitated. He gave TJ his head and pulled the tie on his hat tight as he positioned the glorious sorrel and white lightening marked pinto to overtake Stanwyck once and for all. He planned on running him out to the finish line.

By now, Eastwood had his way with Midnight, and Midnight surrendered in full. The black stallion loved to run and didn't need any heavy prompting from Clint. He just gathered speed like a black steam engine under a ton of coal headed downhill. Midnight remembered his days on *Raw Hide* with Rowdy on his back while he chased strays through arroyos and down steep hills to forest line. Those were the days, and Midnight took advantage of comin' out of retirement to stretch his legs! He was jumping across little gullies and leaping over sage weaving like the cutting genius he was as a top-notch cow horse. If he dropped dead before the finish line, he'd 'a died happy. Clint gave no cause to keep him in gear; there was only one gear and that had a power button!

Of course, Russell wasn't gonna let anybody take the lead. He'd been stretched out a few leagues ahead of the others and Honey loved the speed. She was familiar and confident in this country because it was so like Russell's ranch lands in Australia. He'd brought her over for the *Haul and Box-it*. He heard about it as being one of the toughest endurance races and he just had to give it a try.

Jimmy was pushing Pie. After seventeen years of ridin' together, Pie knew the landscape. In Pie and Jimmy's movies they were usually being chased by Apaches and Jimmy was usually misunderstood by both Indians and sheriffs and robbers and murderers. They were highly skilled at gettin' away, and they had so much experience together that even if they weren't being chased but were in a race they still didn't like being in the rear. Pie and Stewart had one thing on their minds and that was to do the chasin' and pass 'em all, you know give 'em the business, and win!!

So, it was now that these racin' fools were kicked into highest of gears, one neck to neck, others mid-section to mid-section. One would pull back an inch and one would gain an inch. At these full out speeds almost all were cruising between forty-eight and fifty-four mph. The heat of the day had risen so high it smothered the horses and riders, but they kept on. They could see the finish line up ahead about one-hundred and fifty yards. From where they were blasting across the ground they saw a throng of people, so many more than just the town's folks, Elliot, Peckinpah and Devine who were there at the beginning of the race. It was like they'd grown into a population of Dodge City by the way they were spread out across the line. Gosh 'a mighty, thought the narrator. Who the heck are all these yahoos anyway?

Just as the same thoughts crowded the heads of the riders they saw a dark figure on horseback that was big enough that after a few more yards is recognizable, as Boone?! You're kiddin' me thought the narrator, Boone's back in the race, but where'd he come from? He must've got 'round 'em when they were savin' Barbara's behind back at Little Box Canyon Creek. There's just no predicting anything in a story!

"This just isn't fair!" Stanwyck seethed! Now, she was more determined to run Boone and Rafter over if she had to.

For a minute, Midnight forgot about being a steam engine and got a little confused by the out-of-order synchronicity—he'd never even seen Rafter before because he and Clint rode in after all the hullabaloo in the box canyon. It just put him off and he started straining against Clint's handle.

"Shit! Midnight! Don't do this to me now!!" Shouted Clint and tried whipping him with the reins. Midnight was having none of it. Clint did take him out of his retirement just because he couldn't handle a girl on her period, and as he was suffering a small amount of horse dementia these days, what could be done? After all, Midnight would turn forty-some years old in July.

Mortensen and TJ never let up. Their stride was continuous like a mountain sliding down to the sea. He caught up with Midnight and Eastwood and like a bullet from a Winchester rifle sped by so fast Midnight and Clint saw the blur of a brown and white canvas that resembled a cartoon in full speed (think the Roadrunner in *Wily E. Coyote* beep, beep).

Well, that took the sails right out of Midnight. He figured he'd cross the finish line, but in his own damn time. Clint got the message and slowed him back to a dainty canter.

Honey and Crowe saw Boone and Stanwyck and Viggo and Clint. Their minds collected the scene not unlike a kaleidoscope as it made colorful patterns from land, sky, dust, horses and riders. After the terror of the box canyon and the flash flood—not to mention almost getting run down by a green and white VW van in the Indian uprising, Honey had to do everything she could to keep running and trust Russell—even though Russell was having difficulty keeping his mind focused on the race. It was like he was back acting in *A Beautiful Mind* (2001). He was losing perspective and the grueling race was becoming a tricky math problem. He was getting paranoid.

Stewart saw Boone up ahead and sized up the situation. Well, he thought to himself, I can focus on Boone only, or on Barbara and Viggo. It looks like Clint and Russell are in trouble.

Hmm, thought the narrator, wonder what he'll do?

As they all ran for the finish, they could see clearly that there were protesters holding big signs and hollerin' slogans. Then, the riders saw a bunch of riders on horseback. "What the heck," said Stewart who can they be? Pie continued his quest in full run.

Just as Boone looked like he was about crossing the finish line Viggo came roaring in at light speed. TJ was just about run out and couldn't go much further at this pace, but just a few more yards would do it! Rafter eyed the hoards of people with their big lettered signs and heard loud chanting. He spooked and turned up the juice outrunning his time a thousand fold. Boone was taken off guard, and was slopping around in the saddle trying not to lose control. In raced TJ and the two horses and riders were muzzle to muzzle—then a shot went off and all the riders came tearing across the finish line.

"WHO WON? WHO WON?"
"WHO SHOT THE GUN OFF?"
"WHO ARE ALL THESE PEOPLE?"

The clamoring was fierce as the racers bolted through the huge crowd scattering any lingering standers-by that were in the fire line. All the racers and their horses put on the brakes and came breathlessly to a halt, eight pound hearts throbbing. Midnight hung his head almost to the ground he was so spent and it took him a long while to recover and not die right on his feet. Misty Girl was fed up and crow-hopped to unseat an exhausted Stanwyck. Barbara was looking the wrong way when Misty Girl decided to hop the other way. Stanwyck was on the ground unable to get up. Russell and Honey did get across the finish line, but ended up under a stand of Cottonwoods wandering in exclusion until they could get it together.

Viggo and TJ ran straight through the crowd only to stop when they felt free of the cumbersome milieu. So where was Stewart? Yeah, where was Jimmy? He and Pie decided NOT to finish the race and let somebody else take the glory.

"BUT WHY," said the narrator out loud! Did Jimmy know something that we didn't?

It was Peckinpah that stomped up and shouted, **"YOU'RE ALL DISQUALIFIED, YOU IDIOTS! YOU ALL SHOULD'A STOPPED AT THE START LINE!"**

Jimmy just tipped his hat to the two Sam's, Elliot and Peckinpah, and smiled. "I knew somethin' like this was gonna happen, at least suspected it!" And he gave a sly Jimmy Stewart grin.

So why did the contenders not stop at the starting line at the beginning of the race, nobody ever found out for sure, but some things are sure. These protesters had come down from Omak, Washington to be the first to protest the *Haul and Box-it Race*. They were making ready to protest the Omak Stampede in August which held the suicide horse race down the sixty-two degree hillside that was 225 feet long and ended at the banks of the Okanogan River. "Down with animal cruelty," they chanted. "End the Haul and Box-it Race. Stop harming horses!!" This we know for certain happened, but an extraordinary thing took place that day. After everyone settled down they looked around and what they saw will <u>NEVER</u> leave the minds of cowboys and cowgirls anywhere through out time. If there'd been a marquee it would've looked like this!

When this crowd of folks came into focus and the riders saw clearly who all these people were, well they were just dumbfounded!! There were FIFTY of the famous cowboys, cowgirls and their horses to be seen on the Golden Screen and television in the 20th Century.

First time this ever happened at the *Haul & Box-it Race,* or anywhere for that fact! Everybody was whoopin' and hollarin'. There was much laughter and slappin' each other on the back or takin' their hats off to the ladies. Glenn was even there and it looked like he and Tenny survived their near fatal wreck. Both of their eyes were glassy and Boone stood close to them waiting to catch Glenn if he decided to topple. Rory and Domino joined in the uproar that reigned in this reunion. Clint and Midnight were together and stayin' close to Steve McQueen. Even the two Sam's seemed to forget their vigilante hot-headedness. Barbara told Viggo he was too determined, as if she could talk, and Russell was just overwhelmed to be along for a party like this. He couldn't wipe the smile off his face. Boone shouted to Jimmy, "What d'yall say Stewart? Let's all head to the Prickly Pear for a BBQ!"

Jimmy kicked Pie and whipped his hat across his flank. "Meet you there boys and girls!!" Pie cut out vigorously. They all followed Jimmy's lead and turned their mounts toward the Prickly Pear. The thundering of hooves kicked up great clouds of dust that reached almost as high as a skyscraper. The sun was beaming and caught the dust turning it to gold leaving a wide wake of glitter.

PRESENTING

Carey on Mud, Harry Carey Jr. on Billy,
James Garner on movie horse, Roy Rogers on
Trigger, Dale Evans on Buttermilk, John
Wayne on Duke, Audie Murphy on Rebel,
Andy Devine on Joker, Chuck Connors on
Razor, Jay Silverheels on Scout, Chill Wills on
movie horse, Clayton Moore on Silver, Dale
Robertson on Leo, Gary Cooper on Buck,
Gene Autry on Champion, William Boyd on
Topper, Randolph Scott on Stardust, James
Arness on Buck, Joel McCrea on Steel, Slim
Pickens on Dear John, Lorne Greene on Buck,
Steve McQueen on Ringo, Clint Walker on
Brandy, Lee Majors on Charger, Alan Ladd on
movie horse, Peggy Stewart on Smoky, Nell
O'Day on Shorty, Dan Blocker on Chub,
Michael Landon on Cochise, Tim Holt on Steel,
Bill Cody on Chico, Bob "Tumbleweed" Baker
on Apache, Bob "Tex" Allen on Pal, Bob
Livingston on Shamrock, Bob Steel on
Brownie, Buck Jones on White Eagle, Buzz
Barton on Pee Wee, Duncan Renaldo on
Diablo, Fuzzy Night on Old Brownie, Gabby
Hayes on Eddie, Harrymovie horse, Johnny
Mack Brown on Rebel, Leo Carrillo on Loco,
Tex Ritter on White Flash, Tom Mix on Old
Blue, Lash La Rue on Rush, Ben Johnson on
Bingo, Robert Redford & Paul Newman
double on movie horse, Kathy & Margie
Sterling riding double on Brownie , Lee
Marvin on Smoky

BROWNIE AND CLIPPER GO TO CHURCH

For the Episcopal Church in Montana

The curtains in the bedroom blew gently through the open-screened window. Sunday morning was a new day with its promise of blue skies and butterflies. Spring had come early as indeed winter had been weak and pitiful, they said because of the El Nino off the coast of California. It had been weeks of blue skies and sunny days, dropping into the low fifties at night. Drought sat on the aquifer, but to a ten year old girl none of this mattered, whatsoever. Good weather meant she could ride Clipper to church with Grandmother Kit and Brownie. Madison shut hers eyes against the brilliance of a full moon only hours before; light filtered through her eyelids and she saw shadows that looked like a cat's face or squinting just right saw a man with a long coat on. She blinked her eyes open to look squarely into the craters and mountains of the lunar landscape before she felt her body sink into the flannel sheets and snuggly quilts.

Before long, she was awakened by the morning breeze that gently disturbed the gingham curtains and set them whew-wing into her half-sleep dream. Grandmother Kit had told her if it was a good day for riding they could saddle up Brownie and Clipper and ride to church. Smells of breakfast cooking on the stove drifted upstairs as Madison pushed back the covers and pulled her cowboy boots on under her nightie. She slipped out of her bedclothes and threw a cotton dress over her head as she bolted for the stairs.

Kit stood at the cook stove pouring her third cup of coffee. She wore her worn felt cowboy hat. It cocked back on her head and her silvering hair wisped out from under the braided bun that was fixed at the nape of her neck. Her blue blouse accented the Stewart plaid skirt, and she too wore her best cowboy boots for the ride to church.

"I'll saddle up Clipper," Madison said ignoring the steaming pile of pancakes on the table.

Kit eyed her pushing her hat an inch further back on her head, "Oh no you won't. Sit down. The Lord can wait 'till you finish breakfast. So can Clipper."

Grandmother watched Madison pour the syrup like it was free all over her stack of whole wheat cakes and began to devour the sweetness. Kit didn't chastise her, but let her get away with the over indulgence. After a full glass of orange juice,

68

Madison folded her napkin just so, or her grams would make sure she does it right, again. Madison dutifully carried her plate and glass to the sink where her grandmother had a steaming soapy basin of water waiting. She washed her dishes and wiper her hands on the tea towel. Kit was raised by a Victorian mother and had told Madison all about how her great grandmother Catherine believed she was Queen Victoria. She even wore black crinoline dresses which helped with her queenly self-image, and she was fat too. Catherine's influence over her daughter was only partially successful as Kit's personality was a wild card that landed her in Montana wilderness. There were some leftover habits that Grams could never get rid of though. Kit was a real mix, part civilized, part wild fire. She eyed Madison finishing her chore and waved her to go get busy.

Madison didn't catch the screen door and it banged loudly on her exit. Kit let it go. The sun was up at least four inches from the horizon now. It was still a bit chilly. She headed straight for the paddock. As she came around the corner of the building she saw her beautiful Clipper. His black and white coat was losing its winter hairy thatch and turning into the silky body of a Clipper ship with all sails set. The pattern on his coat was the lightening Appaloosa. His white body was streaked with black down his legs and his tail was laced with long black hair mixed, swishing with the white thickness of a true pony tail.

Madison greeted him with "Hey Clipper, its church time!"

Brownie, in his lovely sleek unadorned way, nodded his head because he knew that Kit would come soon to get him ready for church too. Clipper and Brownie had gone to church before. They knew the routine. They'd carry the woman and the girl down through the pasture, turning at the creek to the road that headed south. They'd perk along in a fast walk. Church started exactly at 10. The priest, Mother Elizabeth believed in punctuality, and Madison needed to be vested by a quarter to.

Both men and women are priests in the Episcopal Church. Men were called Father, and women (who weren't allowed to be priests until the 1970's) weren't sure what their title would be so some called themselves Mother, others just Reverend and some just wanted to be called by their first names. Elizabeth chose Mother. This was too confusing for Madison even though it suited Grandmother Kit because she was tired of men running the religious show without women being recognized as spiritual leaders too.

Mother Elizabeth was at least sixty-five, maybe older like sixty-eight. She was soft and cushy with a large bosom that pushed her vestments way out in front. The large gold cross she wore didn't settle on her bodice, but dangled out over the great wall of her chest like it was rappelling down a cliff. Her natural high cheek bones looked lovely with her almond eyes. When you looked into her eyes she'd fix them on yours as if she was saying, come on in. She did like to **genuflect** which is a tradition that is lost in the church today. Every time she passed in front of the altar she stopped like a soldier to salute the flag, but deeply bowed, dropping almost to one knee before she got up to pass the rest of the way. Madison observed her but bent only half as far as Mother just in case anyone was watching.

Grams sang in the choir most Sundays. Her soprano rang out as clear as the swift flowing creek in early summer. Madison loved to hear her Gram's notes lift to the rafters on those Sundays she sang with the high trills of a meadow lark. The two of them were a team. She believed they'd be together forever and ever, like the Lord's Prayer says at the end. Grandmother Kit believed in the spirit world telling Madison that their work wouldn't be finished here on earth. She thought when people died they just stepped through an invisible curtain into a new world where there was plenty to do.

Now, Clipper was ready to worship. He pushed Madison with his big head, his blue eyes looking directly into hers. He'd best be saddled right away, before Grams got there, otherwise, Brownie would push him to the side in his excitement to get saddled first. The pasture was just now springing with little cow flowers, white and tiny. They were popping up all over the place. Bear Creek ran close to the house, and at this time of year flowed full from spring run-off. It ran up the banks to the top of the old cottonwood roots that were exposed in places over the creek bed. Cottonwoods drop their red pods everywhere in spring and when you step in them they stick on your feet. Try pulling them off and they leave sticky red goo.

Madison was named for the great sweeping valley where Grandmother's ranch stretched over two thousand acres in central Montana. A hundred years ago the ranch was much bigger, but chunks of the high mountain terrain were sold to a timber company to get the family through hard times. Really, when grandmother and Madison rode they'd open barbwire fence gates all day and never get off the ranch.

The sun was warm and Clipper was impatient to go to church. He threw his head up and down and pawed the ground. There was no getting him to stop so Madison swung the saddle up on his back hoping he'd settle down. He let his breath out as she lodged her knee on his side to pull the cinch tight. Clipper helped her saddle him up. Grandmother came to the paddock, finally. Brownie watched her as she got the horse blanket from the tack room. He snorted as she threw it up on his back. Brownie's saddle was a Western leather carved beauty. Grams had put silver jingles and all kinds of glitter on that saddle. He eyed it curiously whenever she pulled it off the saddle plank. He acted like he was proud to wear it because when grandmother stepped into the stirrup he sort of danced like he'd found his partner.

Madison swung into her saddle by the time grandmother had gotten the blanket on Brownie. Clipper pushed the gate and Madison leaned over his neck.

"Come on Grams, we'll be late!"

Clipper snorted while Kit threw the jangling saddle up on Brownie, set it just right, and cinched him up. Grandmother tipped her hat giving Madison the sign, grabbed her skirt in her hand and pulled herself up into the saddle. She buttoned her light wool jacket up to the collar and gave Brownie a knee.

They rode through the pasture and took the road in no time at all. The sun was warming them as they pushed toward the church. Grandmother unbuttoned her jacket. All in all the church was about a mile away. The horses competed for the lead walking at a clip. They were on the edge of a trot when Madison let Clipper have his way, with a little kick to be in charge. He broke into a cantor and then Brownie kicked out. Grandmother held onto her hat and let him lope up to Clipper, then they let go into a short gallop, dust rearing out from behind. Madison looked back at her grandmother who was quickly catching up. She loved racing grandmother and she didn't always win, but when she did she felt tall in the saddle.

Before long the church spire was in sight and grandmother and granddaughter reined the two church goers in. They dropped to a trot, then a walk. The silver cross at the top of the spire caught the morning light reflecting the snow-capped mountains of the Madison Range. The new leaves of spring were beginning to protrude from their buds; they were chartreuse and lovely. As the church yard came into view the horses began to slow. A glossy green lawn with a road up to the red doors brought them to a stop in front of St. Ann's Episcopal Church, a modest church that was built almost a hundred years before. It was made out of logs and had six stained-glass windows, three on each side.

Madison and grandmother tied their mounts to the horse posts and headed for the front doors of the church. Madison vested and grandmother joined the rest of the choir. The **processional hymn** began and Madison led the pageant carrying the cross. She had taken two weeks of instruction from Mother Elizabeth to become an **acolyte.** Her long blonde hair accented the bright red of her robes and the white sleeved outer garment called the **chasuble.** She was very proud to wear it, and to carry the cross. Old Mr. Jameson was a cross bearer for over forty years, Mother Elizabeth had told her, so in Mother's mind it was ministry for some folks.

Grams and the choir walked behind her. Kit sang clearly at the top of her soprano from the **hymnal**,

All people that on earth do dwell sing to the Lord with cheerful voice;
Him serves with mirth his praise forth tells, come ye before him and rejoice...

The rejoice holding the A note four counts. They were rounding the second verse when she reached the sanctuary. The choir filed into their stalls just like Brownie and Clipper did when they were turned loose in the paddock to eat their hay.

The prayer to start the service was read and as Ruth James came forward to read the **First Lesson** from the Old Testament Book of **Isaiah** Ronnie Stout, who sweated circles when the sun was out got up and opened the windows. He walked down both sides of the church opening them wide. Ruth's tidy red-dyed hair curled tightly around her face. Her idea of holiness was strict and pious (very un-Episcopalian, but it was rumored she'd been born a Presbyterian).

The notion of her birth was evident when she glared down the children who were giggling and making noise during the service. She was trained long ago and had been a reader for thirty-five years at St. Ann's. One didn't want to cross her or she'd slowly furl her lip upward in a controlled silent snarl, but when she did you know she meant business. For the most part, when Ruth read, people listened, or tried to look like they were. She put her hands on the **lectern** where she had worn down the wood Sunday after Sunday, cleared her voice and began. She hadn't gotten far when suddenly two visitors appeared at the window, just a few feet away from her. Clipper and Brownie got untied from their posts because there they were starring into the church, their bits clumping as they shook their heads. The people sitting in the first row moved down the pew as everyone started to murmur. Ruth glancing up at the sound of disrespect saw those shifty intruders and up went her lip. Her eyebrows twisted and she clutched her fist to her chest. Everyone held their breath not knowing what she would do. She drew in a long sustained breath and shocked them by going back to her scripture reading. She gripped the lectern cleared her throat twice, louder the second time and continued in Chapter 12 at verse 18.

People listened, trying hard lest to press Ruth into another turn of action. The adults pretended that Clipper and Brownie weren't there. Mrs. H. O. Brunney pulled an embroidered hanky out of her purse and held it up to her nose. No one could detect her straight-toothed grin as her eyes stayed straight on Ruth. It was dangerous to look at clipper because his big blue eyes were intoxicating and before long one could find themselves staring helplessly into them. The children sitting so close to the window were dancing in their seats with delight. When they were beginning to get out of control, Ruth would slow way down pronouncing each word syl-la-bic-ally. She was a devil when she was serving her Lord.

She finally made it through the Lesson and somewhere between the **Psalm** and the second Lesson Clipper and Brownie had left the window. The next thing people realized as Ruth entered the Letter to the **Ephesians,** well there they were again! Brownie and Clipper swung their heads in, still on the **Epistle** Side, which is the right side, but at the back of the church. They were chewing grass, some delectable morsel they'd torn from the yard. Brownie kept looking at Grams, but she just ignored him as she knelt during the **Confession of the People**. Madison, sitting next to Mother Elizabeth, watched her grandmother intently. She'd eye Kit then shifting her sights back to her horse she shook her head looking flatly into Clip's eyes. You could see she was thinking, "you bad boy Clipper, when I get a hold of you..." but, she like her grandmother didn't make any effort to get him away from church.

After the Gospel, the two staunch Episcopalian equines had vanished from sight. Just as Mother Elizabeth took her place to begin her sermon Brownie and Clipper poked their heads in just around pulpit level. Now they were on the left side, the **Gospel** side. The window was wide open and they both got their heads well into the room. Mother could reach out and touch Brownie if she'd wanted to. Brownie stretched his neck and nibbled the fringe that hung from the pulpit cover.

Mother laughed out loud and said, "O.k. Brownie, mind your manners. This sermon's for you."

She began. Brownie and Clip could see grandmother now from where they stood. They looked at her then at Mother then craned their necks to see if they could see Madison. Each time Mother talked about love, one or the other cleared their throat in that horsy way, kind of "g-rumph." They'd shake their heads and their manes would tickle down like a xylophone.

When she mentioned the struggle Jesus had in the wilderness, facing off Satan they began to paw the ground and push against the building. When Satan challenged Jesus to throw himself off the pinnacle, for surely God would save him they swung their heads vigorously from side to side, uttering a low whinny. By the time Mother ended her sermon, and Jesus was still fighting off Satan, they were quite agitated stamping their feet and pushing each other around. If the parishioners didn't know better they might think that Clipper and Brownie had been hired as actors by Mother because they sure got her point across.

By the time everyone had gone to the communion rail and the **recessional** hymn began Brownie and Clipper left the window. Madison led the procession down the aisle to the back of the church. When the recessional ended and the final prayer was said, the people shouted, "Thanks Be to God!" To the surprise of everyone the front doors swung open and there was Brownie and Clipper coming right into the church. They got through the big red doors and almost dumped over the baptismal font when Grandmother hooked them by their bridles. Before she could get them to back up Mother walked up to them.

She said, "We owe you a big thank you for coming to church this morning. How did you like my sermon?"

This time even Ruth the elder couldn't snarl down the laughter. You could hear her distraught voice above the howling, "I suppose next time we'll have horses dancing on the altar!"

Clipper and Brownie shook their heads in all directions and whinnied loudly. Mother thought they loved her sermon, but more than anything, they loved Grandmother and Madison. After church when Kit and Madison were riding home, Madison asked her grandmother, "Do you think we can take Brownie and Clipper to church ever again?" Kit felt like they needed to apologize, even though they said they were sorry about the behavior of their horses over and over, and especially to Ruth. Grandmother told Madison she would call Mother Elizabeth and tell her they wouldn't be riding Brownie and Clipper to church anymore and this is what she said.

"You know Kit I've been thinking about this morning and have come to the conclusion that animals are God's creatures too so why can't they be included at church? We live on ranches and as close to the wilderness as possible in these parts so why rule out that you and Madison can't ride Brownie and Clipper to church? I think we can learn a valuable lesson from them. A building doesn't hold God. Everywhere on God's holy earth is God's Country so bring Brownie and Clipper whenever you can. I just hope Ruth survives the decision, and just tie 'em up tighter!

Kit and Mother Elizabeth had a good laugh over that!

Episcopalian Terms of Definition:

Processional Hymn
Acolyte
Chasuble
Hymnal
First Lesson
Isaiah
Lectern
Psalm
Ephesians
Epistle
Confession of the People
Gospel
Recessional hymn

Siege

For the Women of the West

My name is Irma Brighten. I gave birth to a baby girl in the middle of a siege.

William and I had tried to conceive since we were married in 1916 on a rainy day in May, the Sioux Indian month of the "budding moon." I was an anxious and nervous bride with moments of worry, not about the wedding nor even about Andrew as I thought I loved him fiercely enough that we could weather any storm that came our way but there was something in my rearing and most likely my personality that lingered in a dark cloud of doubt: doubt in daily life, doubt in religious life, doubt in my worth, doubt in my purpose. If I'd been a man, I'd of been Thomas who needed proof that Jesus was real when he appeared to the disciples in the upper room. I, like Thomas, would need to insert my fingers into the wounds before I believed with certainty that he was the Lord.

Mother warned me that one day I'd doubt winter, snow, water, and fire if I didn't change my ways, but that was just mother letting go of pooled worry for she was a worrier too and maybe her constant fretting settled into my bones and sinew, eventually. It was most likely a matter of lesser faith than doubt, but I couldn't help it, I was the daughter of a pioneer woman and there was plenty to worry about.

Mother was a reluctant pioneer, but only after she made the arduous journey from Pittsburg, PA to the wilderness of Central Montana. My father needed a woman, a wife to hold him in the night, to cook and sew and bear him children in the mining camp where he staked his claim. She thought she wanted to come west where there was some adventure and there was something about the story he told of his nickname, given to him by the Indians when he first ventured into Sioux country. He was known as "Devil Man with a Gun," as the Indians attacked him and he defended taking two or three out with his Army issued Colt revolver. He gained cautionary respect and was steered a wide berth from then on. She had no idea that her consent to pack up and leave her family home would bring, but who would? Their courtship was short as June was on the horizon and father wanted to make Montana by September. This thing called pioneering was going to be a crash course for mother, but she was young and ready for life. Her parents entrusted her to James Watson thinking that when she left to go west that it might be the last time they would ever see their red-haired quiet daughter again. There were many tears and grave hugs when it was time for departure. The Irish had a wake for a person who was leaving Ireland for the "new world," and it seems appropriate because for the most part, they never did see their loved ones again, at least on this plain, so it was with mother, into the "new world," into the dangerous world, into the world of drafty hand-hewn shacks and smoke-filled rooms and one doctor 30 miles away, not to mention that guns were a part of life. If you refused to handle one, you weren't going to survive.

Mother was afraid of pretty much everything; the darkness of the ten foot by ten foot windowless shack that she and Father lived in during the first winter after they returned to dad's mining claim just outside Diamond City. Snows were aggressive reaching up to four feet drifts around the shack. In the month of the "exploding trees" when the January thaw gave the false impression of spring and tricked Mother Nature (even though Mother Nature can't really trick herself), but with the nature of Montana's winter temperatures dropping to -40F tricked certain trees that had the propensity to jump the gun for an early spring. Hope does not spring eternal for a Mountain Ash, Cottonwood, or Maple during a deep time of freeze and thaw and freeze again. Deadly cold is no friend to human, animal, or tree. Frost bite is a burn and trees experience the same scorching as the consequence of separation of water from air causes a terrific drying, not unlike a kiln. When the sap (life blood) of a tree thaws and then freezes again, it expands putting pressure on the tree bark causing it to split open! This process does not happen quietly, but sounds like an explosion from a fire-arm. This phenomenon scared Mother as she heard the popping trees going off like an arsenal. Father explained it to her more than once, but it didn't seem to matter. "You need to toughen up woman," he'd say to her. He was too busy surviving to have empathy. An explanation should suffice!

Not to Mother. Her fears grew from her constant nightmares of wild animals chewing away at the leather hinges on the one door into the shack. She dreamt of Indians breaking in and dragging her bloodied body through the snow leaving streaks of her entrails along the path to the stock shed while Levinia her milking cow, wailed as she was shot with arrows and hit with clubs. If it wasn't these horrible nightmares, it was the waiting, alone in the creosoted half light of the single oil lamp. Father couldn't be bothered with his wife's fears, and told her so. He'd say she'd have to toughen up again or go stay with Flora Stephens who lived eight miles away. Mother felt foolish and she did begin to adjust to wilderness life as the seasons unfolded. Gradually, her dreams began to hide out in the basement of her imagination. She could pull them upstairs when she needed the adrenaline, and did on occasion.

The law of the land was to survive, to die, or to go insane which many pioneer women did. Mother ended up birthing seven children, five boys and two girls (I am the youngest daughter). She had five at home, which eventually home became a ranch as the mining of gold thinned out and people began leaving in droves, broke or rich. I was the sixth child born so have little recall about mother's birthing methods or knowledge of who came to help out or what her labors were like. When my little brother Archie showed up he came in a white blanket that looked no worse for the wear, but then Mama did have him in Townsend at the hospital. We had neighboring families that we got together with on special occasions, but mostly, there were the old miners holding like a clam stuck on a raven's foot to their grub stakes.

The old fuzzies who stayed on their claims became hermits as women wouldn't have them, neither would soap and water, and socializing became repulsive to them and to their neighbors. One old codger, Ennis McClain, an Irishman was caught in a snowstorm after turning down an invitation by my father to wait it out before he attempted walking the ten miles to his dilapidated, half-built lodge. "No, Arthur, I gotta git goin', old Bennie here needs to git home." When father came in and told us Ennis wasn't stayin' for the invitation he said that Ennis' mule Bennie was pleading with his eyes and a few short complaining brays—it was clear that Bennie was a whole lot smarter than McClain, but there wasn't anything father could do to convince that stubborn Irishman otherwise.

It turned out that the temperature began dropping to around minus twenty and even though father and mother were concerned they weren't going to risk anyone of theirs to go after Ennis until morning. At first light, it was clear that it had snowed a couple of feet during the night. My father and four of my brothers, Art, Luke, Tad, and Archie saddled up their horses to go and look for Ennis. All trace of mule and McClain lay deeply under the snow. They figured they knew the way and if old Ennis kept to the way home, by some miracle that they'd eventually find him. Mother, my big sister Haddie and I packed up beef jerky, a few hard-boiled eggs, and some biscuits for the search.

Our men kinfolk were terribly tough, even though we women were hardening I still doubted the outcome and was worried sick that there'd be trouble. Life to me just brewed along at a topsy-turvy boil. When my spirits dumped, my mother eyed me and watched cautiously to be sure I wasn't found under the covers in bed or sitting in the rocking chair by the fire staring into the flame for too long. After rising in the morning I didn't comb my hair some days. I just couldn't be bothered and what did it matter? Who was lookin' at me anyway? The days when my bleeding came, it was worse. Mama would put me to bed with a hot brick. She understood my menses was mean and double-shifted my chores for me. I could read and we had a few books that got dropped off at the Watson stage-stop when the mail came through town, but there was no reading when my time of month circled 'round. But I would cry, sometimes non-stop, and Mama and Haddie would fret over me patting me and sitting on my bed telling me everything would be all right.

It wasn't until the next afternoon that father and the boys rode up pulling the frozen body of Ennis McClain behind them. After a long and difficult walk through the snow and cold they came upon Ennis who was only about fifty yards from his front door when he dropped down unconscious, and the cold did the rest. Bennie wasn't with them. What often happened if anybody died in winter, they'd be stuffed into a snow bank until spring then they could be buried when the ground thawed. We held old Ennis out by the stock barn until he could be transported to Townsend, about a month.

I didn't come from intellectual geniuses or even political people and as my father put it, "We didn't pick our ancestor's well." We were homesteaders, miners, and ranchers—people of the land who had to scrape by to build a sturdy successful ranching business. Street sense or wisdom of the "now," was effectually present in living out our daily lives back in the mountains where it was a thirty mile horse ride to Townsend, White Sulphur Springs, and about eighty to Helena but making it rich in gold-mining or cattle ranching was just not our bailiwick. We didn't do it for the money. We did it because it was our life.

So it was that before Andrew and I were married, father came down the road one day from Townsend with a brown horse tied to the back of the wagon. He was so doggone brown that his personality was not detectable. I was feeling especially blue that day while I was forced out of my dark shadow to make food for the upcoming wedding. When I saw him ride in, the new pony took my attention and I took advantage of walking out of the kitchen to inspect this new addition. "Who's this father?" I asked.

"Well he's your wedding present, Irma, your very own horse for your new life. I figured you couldn't take Old Jack or Fringe with you so I got you this one. You'll have to name him though. He goes by Knucklehead, but I thought you might want to change that." He smiled.

"Knucklehead, indeed" I scoffed. "Who named him that?"

"Doc's son Randy," father volunteered. "Randy didn't like him much, and I suspect it was the other way round too. When I dropped by to secure the purchase, Knucklehead stood on his foot which created a string of curse words that would light up a fourth of July night. If you asked me, I'd say I saw Knucklehead smile before Randy started hittin' him."

I laughed out loud at the picture in my head. I was gonna like Knucklehead, but I did change his name. Father was more, than not, able to lift my spirits, and he must've known that buying this brown, sturdy mountain pony was just what I needed to believe in as I was fragile in so many ways, except one...I had a dead-eye when it came to target shooting. Don't know why, but I just took to gun-handling, shooting and hitting the mark. My brothers called me Irma Oakley as I competed against them in the fall turkey shoot. I don't want to boast, but it was me who usually provided the turkey for the Thanksgiving table.

I named my pony Brownie because he was so darn brown and besides, it was a good Montana ranch name. I knew other Brownie's on other ranches, but this was his name and that was that. As we got to know each other, we found that we really liked the other. He would wait at the gate in the corral for me, and if it got later than his patience, he'd whinny three times in a row then stop, then whinny three more times. He'd go on like this until I finally paid him attention—sometimes I'd have to be rough sternly telling him "NO boy, not now!" He was more like a dog than a horse. Brownie seemed to know when I was blue; he'd keep up his constant racket until I forced myself to come outside for a ride. I'd saddle him up and grab my .22 rifle (we all had guns and never went anywhere without one. It was the way of the land).

Our ranch was spread out on the west-side of the Little Belt Mountains where the forest was thinner with more pine than fir. There were great meadows for grazing cattle and sheep and the grasses were as plentiful as the Great Plains. Riding into the timber up to the high meadows on Brownie was that Balm of Gilead that my constant changing moods needed. For the most part, I guess I was a mess and functioning normally had become unpredictable. On those rides, I took to shooting grouse with one shot to the head. Shooting a grouse wasn't a great feat because truth be told, you could actually throw a rock at their head and if you missed they'd just wait, almost encouraging you to throw the next one. If you were a good aim, you could bag one every time. I liked pulling the trigger on my .22, so preferred that. Brownie and I became best of friends and as the wedding approached, I felt a twinge of hope.

Andrew and I were married on May 20, 1916 at the ranch. Andrew bought land about ten miles from my family ranch where we'd built our log house and outbuildings to equip our ranching operation. I still fought my moods, daily, but with me being the sole woman on the ranch was expected to do my part. Understanding the ramifications of "not doing my part," I knew that if I was dead weight, then the ranch may fail. If a person ever experienced hard work and depression, well they don't go together very well.

After a particularly long bout, Andrew came to me with no uncertain terms and flatly stated that he was going to get Chante, the Lakota girl living with Reverend Billy and Harriet Swanson in Townsend to come up to the ranch and help me out. I was startled because the firmness in his voice showed a rod-iron determination to make things better for me, and him. There was no objecting and frankly, I thought he was right and felt relief. Chante means heart in Lakota and as little as I knew about the girl she was just fourteen and was an orphan whom Reverend Billy had taken from the Reservation at Wounded Knee when she was little, didn't know exactly what the circumstances were at the time. Chante could read and write English so could read to me during the down times. The more I thought about her coming brightened my spirit.

She arrived two weeks later and settled in quickly. She brought little and she rode a beautiful brown, black, and white paint mare named Olowa, bareback. The appearance of Olowa brought Brownie immediately to the gate, but this time he didn't just stand there whining, but pulled the latch with his teeth to open for a better look. He liked what he saw and came out to greet them.

I wasn't feeling well for a while and after talking with Mother about missing two periods now she confirmed that I must be pregnant. Chante proved to be so much help during those weeks of throwing up and feeling faint that I couldn't imagine not having her here with me. She made sure the cows were milked and the sheep and chickens fed and tended while I made trip after trip to the outhouse to empty my vomit pail and use the privy.

After all of my husband and my trying, we finally had our baby coming. As sick as I was, my depression lifted somewhat with the realization that I would have a baby to love and care for. It always just seemed to be about me; my family was used to see me withdrawn saying each day, how's Irma today? Mother would say, "Well she's been good up until around noon." I was encouraged to be outside in the clean mountain air and to go riding to clear any shadows away. I was always better after I'd gone off by myself, and my sweet Andrew was always so busy with ranch work that I didn't see him until suppertime and after the meal he would make his way back out to finish chores until dark. Having grown up on a ranch, I knew the work cycles through each season, but I couldn't help feel that the busier he was the less he saw me suffering. There had been visits to Doc Smith's in Townsend and his diagnosis was that I suffered from nerves. When women were depressed, a pronouncement of nerves was usually the reason, according to medical science. I was sent home with laudanum, an opiate, to keep me sedated which would hopefully control the crying bouts.

Chante was my savior angel during my pregnancy. For a girl of fourteen, she was kind and smart and a hard worker. We had great affection for each other, and I was always soothed by her singing her native songs in the kitchen or with the animals when she milked the cows. Our budding friendship granted me companionship, a companionship for the first time that did what the laudanum was supposed to do. There were times that Andrew found me humming as I darned his socks or put quilt squares together for the baby blanket I was making.

For those brief moments in time, I was calm.

I'd been married three years all ready. The hardest year was the second summer of my marriage, Father died unexpectedly. He'd been coming back from town after going for six months of supplies when he came to the long hill that eventually straightened out just before the road turned down our drive to the ranch house. Old Jack and Fringe were pulling the overloaded wagon when the right rear wheel gave way pushing the wagon suddenly into the ground. The supplies of one-hundred pound bags of Montana red wheat, beans, chicken feed, building tools, nails, and rolls of barbed-wire spilled to the ground in a crash. Old Jack and Fringe spooked and jumped forward so hard they broke free of the wagon and started running down the hill at top speed. Father was still holding onto the reins when the two horses took off. He was holding those reins so tight, in such a way as to wrap them around his wrists for more control that when Old Jack and Fringe broke loose he sailed right out of the wagon onto the ground behind. He was dragged all the way to the ranch house, about a quarter of a mile. When he was untangled and carried to his bed, the sight of him was the bloodiest mess where most of his clothes and skin had been shredded. He died a week later.

Losing father was terribly hard, on all of us. Mother held her grief close to her chest and continued to dumbly walk through the necessities of the day, not adding any further bad feelings for her children to endure. We all had plenty to deal with, feelings and work. My brothers, especially Art, who was the eldest, stepped into father's role, running the ranch. My sister Haddie moved off the ranch to Helena and got involved in politics.

There was trouble brewing that we weren't aware of and it began last fall. The ranchers in these parts always had ample hay to carry cattle and sheep through winters, but last fall, there was almost nothing. It had been a "dry" year in 1918 and little rain fell in summer. By the end of summer there was no water for irrigation and the springs dried up. We knew that open ranging barely supplied enough forage to keep our stock through the summer and that was only in areas of high elevation and mountains.

Most of us ranchers had no experience with drought as the wild natural grasses were taken for granted. Andrew and my brothers were stockmen of what was referred to as the second phase of stock business and ranch development. My father was part of the first phase. After father's death, and the death of most of the old ranchers from the sixties my brothers and William were without counsel and wisdom which came with the bitter experience of these men of the first phase. The knowledge was simply not available.

We prospered greatly from the war in Europe that led to World War I. Our cattle and sheep business rose to heights of financial boom. Unfortunately, we were like those trees tricked in January after the thaw to believe that we'd have enough grass to feed our stock through the winter. If advice were given, and taken, we would've known we'd be in trouble and should sell our stock in the fall and replace it at a more suitable time, but no one did, and Andrew and I fell into that category.

When the hay was gone, Andrew ended up purchasing all kinds of inadequate feed that had to be shipped from other states at prices far beyond reason. The Great Lakes froze which made things worse and we even gotten taken more by enterprising people who mowed and baled cattails and swamp grass and shipped it out to the west at any price they wanted to ask. What had started as a financial boom last fall turned into a complete bust by spring. When cattle prices fell out from under, the cattle were unsalable. We couldn't make our mortgage payments in the months to come. Our bank held out as long as it could but it finally came to an end when they could no longer support the ranchers, which meant us too. Conditions between us were ordinarily cordial, but the inevitable happened when the strain became too much and the banks had to act. We'd reached a breaking point, and broke. When Andrew met the last time with the banker, the day of reckoning came. After hot words were spoken the banker threw down the gauntlet and handed our overdue papers to the sheriff with orders to foreclose the mortgage.

I was becoming more and more unstable as the situation worsened. First it was the cattle, equipment, horses and other chattel (except for Brownie whom William took to the family ranch) was sold at an auction with five day's notice. They held the sale at our place. The only buyers present were the bank representative and lawyer which meant they took everything from us.

Andrew hired a lawyer who tried to file a declaration of homestead and he advised us to stay in the house and accept the service of <u>no</u> papers. This was the only thing we could do against the bank which was to hold to "Possession is Nine Points of the Law." The bank had somehow gotten the federal court on board and our house was surrounded by no less than six or seven U.S. Marshalls, including the county sheriff and deputies. As long as we were in the house, the law couldn't remove us. The siege began.

Chante was caught with us in the siege. It was the most dreadful of days as we all stayed inside the house, having locked ourselves in. We couldn't venture out to milk the cows or feed or tend our remaining animals. After the first day of no milking our cows began bawling and none of the lawmen took mercy on them. I became more and more distraught and tensions piled on like red ants on a hill of woe. After the second day of confinement the bawling became intolerable and William, Chante, and I decided that Chante should sneak out after it got dark and at least milk the cows and to try to feed the other animals. It was well after ten o'clock when she unlocked the wood-room door to hide along the wall of the house and make her way to the cow shed. We daren't whisper for fear that she would be found out. It wasn't long after she closed the door behind her and we watched her through the window make her way across the yard that she was detected by a U.S. Marshall. She didn't even make it to the cow shed before she got apprehended and taken away.

The commotion of her loud protests was only accented by the crying of the cows and the loud voices of the other lawmen. I sank into the rocking chair with a shudder of grief. I could feel my hysteria building and I started to shake. William was most concerned and told me that he would try to escape in the early morning and go get help. I begged him not to go, but he said there was no other way. He'd go round up Art and at least get somebody down here to take care of the animals. In other words, it was to be decided that I would "hold the fort" until his return in a day or two or however long it would take.

He held me most of the night, but neither of us slept. I was six months along now and the baby was moving a lot lately. That didn't help during a long night of anxiety and fear. Long about 3:30 in the morning William made his break. He was spotted as he hid behind the brush that he thought was good cover. A couple of Marshalls took off after him, but he slipped away from them. He didn't go directly for the family ranch as he thought he'd be apprehended so he made his way to our hay camp about three miles away. How did I know this? We had a barbed wire telephone between the post office and our place, a distance of six miles, and a phone at the hay camp. The phone line was simply the top wire of a barbed wire fence with all splices securely tightened. It worked brilliantly as an improvised telephone devise. William got to the hay camp and rang me up. He told me it might be a few days before he could get back which left me there inside the house. Eventually, the marshals cut the phone line leaving me at bay. Fresh water was about 125 feet away and I dare not go to fetch it. Even though people came to talk to me no one was allowed to leave a message or sending out any note, nor could I send one to them.

I was alone in the house for almost three days when I began feeling poorly. I had enough water to last maybe three more days if I conserved. I lay on the bed visiting the chamber pot every so often; it was on one of those visits when I wiped and found blood tinged with mucous. I wasn't supposed to be bleeding. I still had another three months to go and it was all planned accordingly. Surely, this could not be happening. It was a fluke, maybe because of all the stress that my body was reacting this way. I made my way back to the bed. I could hear men's voices down below me just outside the house. They must be getting tired of this game I thought, surely wouldn't they like to be home with their families? The lawyer insisted that we hold our ground, but for how long, and what would we gain if we did? I mean there were so many of them outside and they obviously had the vantage point. I couldn't even get to the well for water, and that awful bawling. Have they no compassion? Why doesn't any one of them take control of the suffering of my cows? The walls in the house were beginning to close in on me with each agonized hour that passed. "So help me" I spoke aloud, "I could just murder everyone of 'em, the bastards!" I surprised myself with the thought that I'd even sworn. Swearing was for crude men, but here I was swearing as the walls and my surroundings became a prison, a prison to starve me out. How could Andrew let it come to this? "Mother, please come. I'm scared to death!" My body was doing strange things. As hungry as I'd been, I was even thirstier. The water was so low and in the June heat it tasted lifeless. My back was aching and I couldn't get it to stop. I tried rolling from side to side, standing and bending, stretching. I held onto a chair and moved my hips around, but that only seemed to make it worse. I'm scared, but I will not cry out for help or leave my home. Andrew expects me to stay and hold which I will, but I just want Mother. "MOTHER" I cry out and groan as the pain is worse. This time the aching turns sharp like a knife penetrating my abdomen. It comes and I gasp as I roll on the bed holding my stomach. The pain comes and then goes and comes and goes and each time it gains momentum as it becomes searing hot and I can't breathe, I can only groan and cry, but not even enough time for that. In one moment, all of a sudden, I cry out and out pops my baby almost to its chest. I feel it between my legs and don't know what to do. Then another pain and its small body slides out onto the sheet. Blood and water are drained from me. "MOTHER!" I screamed and even then no one surrounding the house, if they even heard me came to my rescue. No, I was alone with my baby. I got the courage to pick it up and look at it. It was a girl and she wasn't breathing. There was nothing instinctual to do. I had nothing, no sense, no knowledge, and no animal reasoning. I just stared at it. The baby was still attached to me by its umbilical cord and if it hadn't been for the giant pain that made me push out the afterbirth we would have been locked in a death embrace. I lay back on the pillow panting and then I lost consciousness.

I awoke in the dark feeling the dampness of the sheets. The baby was cold and I was cold and the night was cold. "William," I cried out losing his name weakly. Then I wanted Mother. Her name is Marie I heard in my mind, call for Marie— "MARIE" I cried out! There was only silence and the pounding of my heart. Another day came and went as I woke and fell unconscious and woke dazed and fevered. There was no movement from anyone to check on me and in my frame of mind I saw the monsters that kept me prisoner. It was sometime during those days that I managed to work out what I must do with my baby's corpse. I was almost beyond crying because the situation was so dire. What little strength I had I fumbled with the blankets trying to wrap my baby up. A desperate thought came to me. I should wrap the baby in the finished quilt and put it in the stove where I would set it afire and burn it up. I could not bear to not do something and in my fevered mind saw a funeral pyre. I had to get this baby burned up. I tried lighting the wood and for a few moments it caught fire before I collapsed on the floor. When I awoke, I was so cold that I crawled back into the bed. It was then that I made sure that the guns that William had loaded were right next to the bed. I pulled the Winchester repeating shotgun up on the bed and made it ready to use if any of those monsters found their way in. William set the 35 caliber Remington automatic rifle fully loaded on the side of the bed before he left and on a small stool he'd placed a 32 automatic pistol, fully loaded.

It was the eighth day of the siege. William finally found his way to the family ranch where Mother was crazy over me. Art had just returned from a few days away and she came flying out the front door yelling that she had to see me, no matter what they said, she was going! Of course, William did not stand in the way, as he too was crazy with fear that I might not even be alive. I had given up all hope and was more unconscious than conscious until I heard voices outside the house that were NOT my captors. It sounded like a scuffle was going on because the marshals had surrounded Mother, Andrew, and Art trying to block them from going into the house. When I heard their voices, I screamed as loud as I could, "Marie! --- Mother!" Irma's mother panicked and cried out. "Irma, are you all right?" I yelled back disoriented, "Yes, I'm all right, but I wish someone would come and get this dead baby!"

William turned to the head marshal and defied the law by telling him to shoot him in the back but by god he was going into the house! The marshal stood shocked at this outcome and moved away to let him by. The door was locked, and Art jumped forward to break the door down. When the lock broke, William was on his way upstairs in front of everyone. Art shouted to William, "Be careful William, you know she's a dead-eye with a gun." No one who crossed the threshold of that door would ever forget the odor that permeated the house. It was a smell that would never go away. When I was discovered, Andrew fell to his knees beside me and I didn't even recognize him. I fought like a wild cat like it was a nightmare and the monsters were coming in on all sides. Mother came to me then, holding me and weeping and soothing me. I grew calmer but it took a long time for me to calm. They had to search for the baby and when they found her half-burned up in the stove they could only imagine what I'd been through.

They got Doc Smith and two nurses to come out to the ranch where the nurses stayed, and with mother's love and direction, for two weeks until I could recover. I cannot tell you much of my recovery. My family buried the baby and William and I ended up losing the ranch. I insisted that we sue the bank and we won $15,000, but the bank appealed the case and we ended up settling at our lawyer's advisement getting only $2,000 dollars which paid most of it to the lawyer. There was one silver lining in our dark experience and that was that it was discovered that 160 acres had unintentionally been omitted from the mortgage. This we salvaged from our tragedy. Most of the acreage was in meadow land and it was here where I lost William while he was mowing hay in 1938. He died of a heart attack.

I clung to my little piece of mother earth after William died and have been successful in building it up to close to 1,500 acres. I own up to 100 Hereford cows; I swear I know every cow by name and the name of their ancestry. I owe no one and still run my own spread. I am 83 years old.

The Summer We Lost Mother

For Mother

Kay and Charlie finished the morning dishes leaving the dish towel more damp than necessary, but they were in a hurry to get out into the June sunshine and didn't wait for the dishes to drip. School was out now and they were free, free to play like an eleven and eight year old should all summer long. Their farm lay just outside Manteno, Illinois where their dad was a dairyman with about fifteen head of the most beautiful black and white Holsteins you ever saw. He milked each cow every morning and every evening, by hand. His calloused hands were strong and his grip could hold iron in one fist. The children had a game where their father would flex his muscle like a strong man and then they would grab onto it like it was a jungle Jim and swing back and forth, back and forth. He was lean and his body was filled with work. At the end of the day when he had finished milking and the sun was floating on the rim of the earth they could hear the backdoor screen slap the door-jam and the water being turned on in the deep sink on the porch. Father would roll his sleeves way up on his arm and begin washing his hands all the way up to his elbows. He would wash and wash until the blonde hair on his arms was as soft as down. Once he was satisfied that he had scrubbed off what seemed to be at least a layer of skin he would come into the kitchen and take a plate of food that mother had kept warm for him in the oven for supper.

Kay was three years older than her brother Charlie. They were of German descent and were fair blondes with blue eyes and sculpted bone structure. Farm life kept them healthy as mother baked bread and picked beets, carrots, lettuce, turnips, and cabbage from her large garden. She spent hours in the big kitchen canning and processing food for winter. A Monarch woodstove sat inside a huge fireplace and when November came the children hung their mittens and snow pants up to dry on large hooks. Their mother hung clothes over a line in the winter that father had rigged above the stove. Everything worked hard on the farm--the tractor, the backhoe, the milking utensils, pails, garden hoe, shovel, wood saw, and an endless assortment of all kinds of tools that the Industrial Revolution had spawned from its new-found inventions. Father still milked the cows by hand as he had yet to save enough money to buy a

Mehring milking machine. Until his bank account became more robust he would just have to keep using his large strong fingers for grabbing the teats then grasping them fully pulling down squeezing until the milk jettisoned into the pail causing the sound of an empty pail to ring and a filling pail to swoosh. Mother and Father worked from sun-up to sun-down and when they finally pulled the covers up in the last waking moments of the day, the blessed calm of night swept in like a giant hand, a hand unlike father's, but like mother's: soft and soothing, warm and comforting.

Mother had flaxen hair that almost reached her waist. When she put on her emerald green robe and sat in front of her vanity brushing her hair Kay would watch the thick tresses catch the light and she imagined she was a spider that could enter between the strands finding protection hidden deep within the tendrils. When mother brushed her hair, Kay felt safe. Kay's hair was flaxen like her mothers, and she had plenty of it. Her father cut her bangs short but mother insisted that she wear it long, in braids or a ponytail. Every Sunday just before church her mother would heat the curling tongs and do some fancy curls on Kay. By two o'clock in the afternoon the curls would straighten out and she'd look like she looked on Saturday and the rest of the week, but mother tried on Sundays to take the ordinary out and put the celebratory in.

Hair was somewhat of a phenomenon in their family. Father's was thick and golden and he wore it cropped short. It grew like crazy and mother had him sit in a chair in the kitchen every other Saturday to cut it. She was really good at cutting hair and got a hold of Charlie too. The thick dense hair was a family pride. When Grandmother

Catherine had passed mother's sister Julia had cut a swath from the top of her head and Kay used to get it out of the top drawer of her aunt's bureau to unwrap it from its hanky where it lay quiet and undisturbed. The piece was extremely thick and was white with a tinge of blond. Why this remnant of Kay's grandmother fascinated her she couldn't say, but hair became, like in all stories that she had heard, a central theme, one to be announced by an author as if a character had no identity without it. She remembered her father reading passages of the *Iliad* to her and she imagined Helen of Troy's hair above all other description. Her love of horses may have been at the source of hair, relating Helen's high ponytail that cascaded down her back in a romp of gorgeous perfect curls to her beloved horse Brownie. His mane was dark brown the same as his coat and tail. Brown blended over him as it beat out white or black or sorrel. Brownie was perfectly, uniformly, and totally brown.

She loved her mother as much as she loved Brownie who was a constant companion throughout her life. He was foaled the same year that Kay was born in 1925. Brownie was a three year old when her brother Charlie came into the family. Kay's father had first put her up on him just around the time Charlie was born. He would lead Brownie around the corral with his little girl sitting as light as a small wren on his back. Brownie was the most wise and gentle horse, even as a two-year old. He just knew that this fragile little creature was his charge and he treated her like she was an unbroken egg balanced on his back.

Brownie had this look he'd give whenever the kids approached the paddock. He would be eating and in mid-chomp he would hear them chattering and turn his head like horses often do when they are curious, but Brownie never went back to his munching. Once he knew they were coming he would swing around and face the paddock gate. Once his eye fell upon the tykes, he would move toward the gate, his neck outstretched to meet the first little hand that reached up to feel his velvety nose. Kay and Charlie climbed up on the gate and almost always had an apple or carrot or some delectable treat, but often Brownie ignored the offering just to nibble at their little fingers. They would squeal with delight when they felt his bristly chin hairs brush their skin and his lips curling around their knuckles. His mother, Dixie Jingle who resembled Brownie, but was darker brown, the color of seal fur, would whiny low and swing her head up and down. She had taught Brownie goodness just like Kay's mother had taught her gentility. Mother was always quietly good natured and had a subtle sense of humor. She would bake gingerbread cookies and playfully add another arm or leg to the figures. It wasn't unheard of that she'd build two heads on a cookie, and the children who painted them with bright frosting giggled and made a game when it came to eating them--which head would be bitten off first.

Mother had three sisters, Aunt Gertie, Aunt Esther, and Aunt Julia. Julia and Esther didn't come to visit much to the farm as they both lived north in Chicago, but Aunt Gertie, who was mother's favorite sister lived in Manteno and she and mother would meet every time mother went to town for shopping or church or lunch. Gertie often visited the farm as it was only a few miles out of town. Her real visiting day was on Sundays though.

She'd come for Sunday dinner and she and mother would sit and play Canasta all afternoon.

One of these Sundays the family was sitting around the kitchen table enjoying a roast beef supper when the backdoor screen started to hit the jam with punctuated slams of wood on metal. Father got up to secure it and after he did he came back into the room his forehead furrowed. He announced an impending storm coming in from the north and knowing that northerlies meant business he told everyone to take a last bite and head for the basement. Just as soon as he got the command out of his mouth, a deafening crash came followed by a series of cracks. Mother sat up abruptly and shouted at the children to get down the stairs, now! Kay, Charlie, and Aunt Gertie didn't hesitate another second but hopped out of their chairs and hurried, Gertie pulling up her long skirts to run to the basement stairs. They threw open the door and the four of them filed quickly down. Father wasn't right behind them because he noticed that after the cracking went off that an electrical unit just out beside the house flew into pieces and a streak of fire and sparks shot out of the pole throwing glowing shrapnel up against the house and roof. The wind seemed to suck the air out of the house and he got down on all fours and crawled along the floor pulling his body to a front window so he could see what was happening.

An eve along the roof was glowing and a hint of smoke began to grow as the wind blew life into it. It began to billow out and it was then that father knew the roof was catching fire. The rains were right behind the wind and he thought to himself that maybe they would put the fire out, but he wouldn't wait long enough to take the chance that it didn't. In spite of the terrible raucous of storm wind he decided to go outside and try to put the fire out. He called down the stairs and told mother and Gertie what was happening and that they should stay put unless he told them otherwise and dashing out the back porch door into a raging wind where debris was flying in all directions, he made his way round the house to where the power line had blown apart. The fire in the roof was mostly smoking, and for a minute father had to figure out how he could get to it without being blown into the next county. He did something very clever. He found a milk container that lay along its side and pulling it up straight yanked the lid off cutting his fingers. Inside the pail was a rope that he kept dry. He pulled at the rope and it unraveled on the ground in front of his feet. He then tied the rope to a galvanized pail near by, scooped it into the cattle water tank and with all his might swung the rope around his head gaining cylindrical force that held the water in the bucket. Faster and faster the bucket picked up speed then he let go just as the bucket reached the elevation of the roof where the smoke was pouring out. The pail hit the eve and spilled out its contents splashing water against the house.

The wind continued to howl. Blood was dripping down his forearm from the cuts on his fingers. He ran to grab the bucket and repeat the procedure when he heard his daughter yell out to him that she was there to help him. He yelled at her to "Get back into the house!" Kay did not obey her father, but stood behind him not budging. Off in the house they could hear mother screaming for Kay to get back inside. She stood there holding herself against the wind, her dress blowing in all directions like a mad woman's eyes darting about. Father could not stop to discipline Kay, but yelled through the wind to get another pail immediately and fill it full of water from the trough. This time Kay did as she was told and ran, fighting the gale, to the back porch where she found another work pail. She brought it to her father and he tied the rope around it and let it fly, the same as before. The pail hit the roof pouring water into the smoke. Kay understood to grab the other pail and prepare it for yet another swing at the fire in the roof. Father took the third pail repeating the throw. Just as the water blasted against the roofline it began to deluge. The heavens opened up and a solid sheet of water drenched everything to an inch of its life. The roof became sodden and the smoke and fire was doused. Father picked up Kay and ran to the backdoor where he struggled to keep it from smacking them senseless as they darted through.

When Kay and father gained cover, they stood staring at each other as pools of water rushed off their clothes onto the floor. He dropped to his knee and reached out to pull her into his arms. His hand was bloody, but it meant nothing in that moment. As he grasped his shaking daughter, he heard mother calling from down below. It was then that father said, "Why Kay, why didn't you obey me and go back into the house?" Kay's heart was heard in her ears as it pounded like the heart of a dinosaur. She opened her mouth to speak and what came out was low and scared. "I was afraid. You might not come back. I'm sorry father, I'm sorry..." her voice became limp as she fell into her father.

Mother heard talking and bolted up the stairs. When she saw her husband holding Kay tightly and the blood on her dress she gasped and shrieked "What's happened Charles!!? Oh my god! Kay!" Father held his bloody hand up shushing his wife. "She's ok Maudie, she's ok. It's my blood." Charlie and Aunt Gertie followed mother to the porch. It was Charlie, when he saw his sister drenched to the bone and his father holding her close to him like a wounded fawn, and then the blood; he started to cry. Mother turned to him and opened her arms. He flew into them and reached out for Kay and father.

After the storm passed, and father's fingers were cleaned and bandaged did the family sit down to talk about the storm. Kay sat with mother on the divan. Mother couldn't stop petting Kay and when she tucked her under the covers that night she put her hand on her forehead and her hand was cool. When Kay looked into her mother's eyes she saw the reflection from the oil lamp. It seemed to fight the darkening shadows that Kay somehow perceived the storm had brought.

Kay couldn't say when it happened, but she noticed changes in her mother in mid-summer. After the storm she began to neglect the vegetables in the garden, leaving them to over-ripen in their neat rows. Kay watched her in the garden, but instead of picking she found her squashing the tomatoes under foot, leaving their juices to seep helplessly into the earth. It was so unlike her mother who never wasted anything around the farm but tediously cut out every bruise in a fruit and salvaged cabbage leaves and stems of broccoli for stews and soups. She was a stickler about waste and Charlie and Kay were never allowed the luxury of leaving their plates filled with uneaten food.

Mother's fastidious way of washing clothes and hanging them on the line to dry was fascinating to watch. Kay would hold the pin bag and hand her mother pins. She was deliberate when it came to pinning clothes up. A shirt had to be pinned just at the shoulder seam. The sheets were hung as if they were a parachute, not folded over the line but pinned up on one side, then taking the other end of the sheet she'd pin the opposite side on the other line leaving the cloth to flutter like a jib in the wind.

Kay wasn't exactly sure when she started noticing the clothes left heaped and overflowing in the clothes baskets or when mother stopped putting father's dinner in the oven at the end of a day but she began hearing her father ask his wife what was wrong. She didn't answer, but muttered under her breath, her hands gesticulating as if she were talking to a crowd. When he dared to complain or ask why, she often turned her back on him. More and more he stopped pressing her. She didn't comb her hair anymore and sat in the shadow of the bedroom door for hours. She sat in unchanged clothes that were often wet from pee and her beautiful hair was snarled and matted hanging limply down her back. When the children came to get their hugs, she pushed them away talking in gibberish. Charlie would cry when his mother denied him her warm secure arms. Kay would put her hand on his shoulder and direct him away from her.

The change in her mother happened gradually that summer, like water let out of a beaver dam slowly. One afternoon, Kay was chasing Charlie through the washroom when she stopped like a horse on a dime at her mother's back. Her mother stood staring out the window, her hands starched straight against her stained blue cotton work-dress. When Kay softly called out "mother," her mother jerked her head around staring at her daughter as if she didn't know her. Kay took a sudden step backward, overturning a wash pail. As it clanged on the stone floor her mother startled by the noise suddenly rushed past her pushing Kay into the wall hard.

She didn't tell her father about the incident as it was one of many strange things that were happening with their mother. Charlie was Kay's only playmate and they found themselves staying away from Mother and the house more and more during the day. Father continued to take care of the cows, milking them like clockwork, but he was different now. He wouldn't offer his strong arm to swing on as he always did; he would make his way to the house not stopping when Kay and Charlie were playing in the yard. His once gentle and kind nature made way into impatience and he spoke sharply to Kay and Charlie when they would begin bickering while he was in the middle of milking. He refused to be interrupted, but seemed propelled in a straight line to get his chores done. As much as he stayed within the routine of the daily chores he vanished outside the routine becoming a nervous husband, always watching over his wife as she became more and more of a stranger. His sharp light blue eyes carried a shroud of pain in them as a neglected cow might look whose owner stopped feeding it.

Summer left July into August and Kay and Charlie took to riding Brownie everyday, for hours. They would bridle him and climb on his strong Morgan back from the fence at the paddock. Father taught them how to ride and felt completely confident about letting them ride Brownie without him watching over them.

Every morning the children would finish their chores, skirt mother who sat in her room behind the door and go find Brownie who was always waiting for them. They rode bare-back. Kay usually sat in front with Charlie holding onto her waist. Sometimes she let Charlie ride in front so he could learn how to steer Brownie, even though everyone knew that Brownie knew exactly what he was doing with these little ones and would never let them steer him into some unforeseen danger.

The farm was laid out on a grid of country roads. If you rode down the drive through the entrance to the farm you could turn left and head about 3.7 miles you'd find yourself at the outskirts of town. If you rode right you'd go about a mile where the Manteno military cemetery lay with its straight rows of small stone grave markers that looked insignificant to passers-by. Brownie often took the children past the cemetery where just a road beyond he turned into a large corn field. In the heat of the summer afternoon the children would find themselves rocking from side to side as if their mount was a camel in the desert, their short legs spread as wide as they could go. Brownie methodically and carefully would find two wide rows of corn to walk between. In August, the corn was higher than Brownie's head. The horse and riders were hidden from view as they secretly passed through the tall-green leaved corn stalks. When the day became muggy and flies began torturing them they found relief in the cool of the shade. The stalks, with their many leaves brushed the horse as he passed along dissuading any nasty black flies with red eyes to bother him or his riders.

Small beads of perspiration would appear on the foreheads of Kay and Charlie as the sun beat down on that growing corn. When they reached the edge of the field Kay would jump down and help her little brother slide off of Brownie's glistening back. All three friends would stand in the shade of a feral apple tree and take a drink of cool water that Kay brought in her school thermos. The children picked the August wild flowers and lay on their backs, knees up watching the clouds billow into ships at sea or angels watching from heaven.

Sometimes they would play a little game imagining that mother was walking up to them through the corn rows. Kay always wanted to play this game even though Charlie usually wanted to play cops and robbers, but she somehow always talked him out of it saying, "Oh look, here comes Mama with a basket filled with bread and butter and currant jam." He fell for it every time. Kay imagined that she wore her apron as if she'd just come straight from the kitchen to find her children. There at the edge of the steamy corn field Kay would order Charlie to lay out the pretend bright festive picnic blanket and lay their freshly picked bouquet filled with pink petals from wild petunia, bright yellow black-eyed Susans, purple Asters and spiky Bee Balm in the center. They would sit among the tiny Buttercups and watch a Swallowtail with its black and yellow regal pattern flit from flower to flower. Mother would sit with them and tell them stories about when she was young and lived in Canada. This is the game Kay wanted to play about mother. She thought that if they made their natural hide-a-way soft and beautiful that she would come and find them.

It happened a few times that last month of summer when Brownie turned left at the gate rather than right. He had to be more careful along the road to town. It wasn't that the road was busy, but it was a thoroughfare for the farmers and often the Boswells would pass Brownie and his charges in his buckboard which was pulled by Saint and Josephine, his two hearty Belgians. Brownie heard them coming and would pull far over to the side, almost walking in the ditch. The children would wave as Mr. Boswell tipped his hat. Kay and Charlie were a familiar sight to all the neighbors, especially that summer.

Many long hours were passed along the irrigation ditch at the edge of the corn field. One might say there were happy moments as the farmhouse with all its bad feelings was far away. When it was time to go back Brownie whinnied to the children. There was an old tractor sitting rusted nearby. Brownie would walk over to it and wait for the children to climb up so they could reach his back. Charlie's short little legs had a harder time getting on so Kay would boost him up in front first, then swing herself up behind him.

Aunt Gertie was often at the farm those hot summer afternoons now that mother was sick and she would stand in the yard calling to the children as she saw the sight of a brown horse with two bobbing heads come down the road and turn into the gate leading to the house. She usually had supper waiting for the tired riders. After Brownie was un-bitted, given a good amount of oats, and left in the paddock with Dixie Jingle Kay and Charlie headed in to wash up with father. He was a loving man, and even though he had one more round of milking to do would meet them in the wash room for a supper scrub. He no longer expected his supper after his chores were finished, but thankfully took his sup with the children and Aunt Gertie. The four of them talked about the children's adventures around the table. Father was fine with them going down to the road, but going to town was forbidden, and Brownie and the children knew it.

The town of Manteno is a small farming community with churches, a mercantile, school, a little library, and a café. It was settled in along the moraines where rocks and soil had once been deposited by glaciers, millennia ago. The little community sprang up at an "end moraine" where in its case a low hill was formed as it ran perpendicular to the direction of ice movement. These hills were formed at the end of a glacier when the ice melted. The plain began to run out away from the moraine and flattened the land in the direction of the farm. It sat juxtaposed to the moraine as it ran up behind it just behind the milking barn. It was hard to imagine that once this was glacial country as looking out over the gentle landscape, one could not imagine ice sheets covering the earth here.

About a mile from the house the road passed by a place where acres and acres of land were filled with huge buildings, some just being built. It looked like a huge factory on the outskirts of a town. The brick buildings reached stories into the sky and had massive wings that stood out in sections from each other. The place bustled from dawn until night-fall with workers and people coming and going. The road to town passed right by this monolithic phenomenon, and it became an adventure, like going to downtown Chicago because it was exciting to watch the continual construction activity. When Brownie turned left on the road to town his hooves struck the dirt road in harmony with hammers pounding and the scraping of mortar from bricks being placed one after the other up the walls of one-hundred buildings.

As the children and Brownie walked down the road they looked west across a large field to see three very large buildings completed. If one went up in an airplane they would see that the buildings looked like huge H shapes. They were all made of red brick and stood two stories high. If one looked across the great field and kept walking down the road north soon other buildings would come into sight. There seemed to be a wide road in front of the H shaped buildings. It eventually became obscured by smaller buildings on the west side of the road, and when they dared to ride further toward town they came to another wide road that led to an important looking building, like a post office or a school and even though the road led into the compound from the rear the building still looked highly esteemed with a tower and cupola reaching high into the air. If you were around front and standing on the stairs looking out you would see a long boulevard that reached a few blocks past the H buildings and stretched all the way out to the power station that lay at the end of land.

There was a large sign just at the turn at the entrance to the back road that said *MANTENO STATE HOSPITAL*. Kay and Charlie didn't know exactly what kind of hospital it was, but thought maybe it was for people who couldn't go to Chicago if they needed to.

It wasn't often that Brownie decided to turn left after leaving the farm, but when he did the children grew excited wondering what new thing was happening at the hospital that day. Otherwise, as summer was drifting into late August and school was just on the horizon, the field corn still needed at least two months to dry on the stalk before cutting; harvesters brought in their machines which gobbled the stalks to spew out corn for the livestock market. Now Illinois sweet corn was usually harvested in late July and August and couldn't be duplicated anywhere else on earth, or at least that's what father always said, and Kay and Charlie knew he was right because when Aunt Gertie served up a pile of corn for supper sometimes that was about all they ate. It dripped with butter and a little salt and pepper down the children's chins and as it popped off the cob it exploded into sweetness and lingered around their tongues until the next bite, which came immediately after the last one found its way to the pleasure centers that humans have just for sweet corn. Charlie could mow through a cob in seconds, and sometimes Kay would time him.

In spite of what was happening to Mother, Father and Aunt Gertie tried to keep life as stable and comfortable for the children as possible. The summer was coming to a close. Brownie knew that the children would be leaving the farm to go to school soon and somehow he knew that Mother was not doing very well. Often horses will figure something is not right and try to compensate for it. Brownie knew that sometime he would be asked to do something for Kay's mother. He just didn't know when or what. He stayed to his daily riding with the children keeping more to the roads rather than into the fields and often he and Dixie Jingle would stand head to tail swishing flies like horses do. Father was using a tractor these days around the farm so Dixie Jingle was more like a family pet than a worker. She used to pull the wagon in past years and still did on occasion, but mostly she was retired now. No matter how gentle she was, Kay and Charlie never included her in their rides as they liked to ride Brownie together and go alone.

August turned into September. The children went back to school. They rode Brownie to the end of the drive where he would deliver them to the school bus driver. When they got on the bus and waved good-by, Mr. Collins would rev the engine and pull away from the driveway. Brownie would watch the dust as the bus disappeared down the road toward town. He would then turn and walk back to the house. He looked for Mother outside, or through the window. He thought he saw her once, but she was like a ghost that passed like vapor on glass. He waited for her to come out of the house, and when she didn't he would turn toward the paddock. He'd let himself in through the gate after drinking a draft of water from the tank at the fence.

School days came and went. The air changed from humid and hot to cool mornings, with warm afternoons. Gravenstein apples in the orchard turned rosy and enormous waiting for Mother to pick them. Instead, they started falling to the ground sinking into the un-mowed grass. Worms and yellow jacket wasps loved them. The longer they lay on the ground they softened making it easier for decay.

The days became shorter and evening fell early. The nights would become long and shadows leaked out of the corners into the light. Mother kept to her room, or perhaps she was kept in her room by

Father because now she was rarely seen. The house felt haunted without her. She was there just in the next room, but for the strange sounds they were not allowed to see her or be with her. Kay would leave the confines of the house in the evenings to find Brownie who she found lying down in his stall sometimes. When she found him like this she would lie next to his warm body and holding on to his neck would cry for her mother. He made a soft sound in his throat, trying to comfort Kay. Father would have to come and get Kay for bedtime. He tried to comfort her too, but fell short. He just didn't know what to do or say to his daughter.

One night after Kay and Charlie had been asleep for awhile she was awakened by arguing downstairs. She heard thumping coming through the floor above the bathroom. Kay held her breath and listened as hard as she could. She could hear father's voice commanding her mother. She threw back the covers and stole out of the bedroom to the stairs. The sounds got louder and even though she felt her heart beating like a great drum she slowly walked down each stair quietly. She could see that the door to the bathroom was open and her father's shadow fell against it. Kay heard her father command his wife, "Put the razor down Maude!" as she struggled against the weight of his body. He held her arm at the wrist while she fought him screeching that she had to "KILL THE CHILDREN!!" God told her she had to "KILL THE CHILDREN!" "NO-O-O-O, LET GO! I HAVE TO KILL THE CHILDREN---LET ME LOOSE!" She hit and kicked him trying desperately to keep possession of the razor. He finally was able to subdue her by straddling her against the wall and squeezing her hand so tight that she was forced to drop the blade onto the floor. She immediately collapsed with all of her weight dropping to the floor as she tried to scramble to pick up the razor blade. He took the advantage and pinned her down. Her head hit the tub and she lay dazed. In the next moment, she went limp, and panting like a panther after a thwarted kill Mother lost herself to exhaustion.

Kay was standing almost at the door of the bathroom when Father saw her and half-shouted, "Kay you have to call the doctor. Do it now!" Kay looked at her mother lying breathless and exposed on the bathroom floor. Father saw her taking it in and repeated, "Kay! Go now, call the doctor." She fled to the telephone on the kitchen wall, picked it up and spoke to Eleanor the operator to get Dr. Whitney immediately! It was an emergency! When the doctor answered the call she told him to come out to the house, her mother had fallen and hit her head on the bathtub. What seemed an agonizingly long time, about forty-five minutes Dr. Whitney finally knocked on the door. Father was holding his wife in the bathroom while Kay had sat on the stair waiting.

She was numb with confusion and could barely speak to the doctor upon opening the door for him to come into the house. When he did he took off his hat and carrying his medical bag went directly into the bathroom where Father was holding Mother. He began to examine her. Father got up and left the room long enough to tell Kay that she needed to go in the kitchen and put the kettle on for tea. Kay obeyed her father and was glad to have something to do.

She could hear the doctor and her father talking softly, "What's happened here Charles?"

Father told him that his wife had taken razor blades out of the medicine chest and was going to use them to cut the children's throats in their beds. Dr. Whitney was astonished and asked him if he knew why. Father said, "She heard a voice telling her to kill them. She said it was God who told her to kill them." His voice became low and he said she'd put up a big fight and she fell to the floor hitting her head on the tub. The doctor said, "How long has she been acting like this Charles? Father thought it had been awhile since his wife had taken to strange behaviors, and he couldn't understand it, but it wasn't an illness that he felt he could get help for. He tried to manage it himself with the help of mother's sister Gertrude. This was the last straw and now that Dr. Whitney was involved something had to be done.

After Mother was examined in the bathroom the two men carried her to the bedroom where Dr. Whitney gave her a strong sedative. She had a nasty bump on her head. The doctor told Father to watch over her the rest of the night and that he would be back first thing in the morning to talk about a course of action.

When he left, Father turned toward the kitchen. Kay was sitting at the table waiting for the tea to steep. Finally, when Father came to her she saw his face which was pale with sunken eyes. His shoulders drooped as he walked to sit next to her. He sat and looking directly into her eyes, took her hands and couldn't speak. He dropped his head to his chest and let out his breath while tears streamed down his face. She pulled her hand away from his and touched him on the cheek. He pulled her onto his lap and hung on to her tightly.

In the morning the doctor came back. Kay and Charlie were getting ready for school. Father told Charlie that his mother wasn't feeling well was why the doctor came so early. Charlie had slept through the terrible night so was bouncy and anxious to catch the bus. Father told Kay not to tell him anything about what had happened, which she knew in her heart and mind that it would accomplish nothing, so she protected her little brother by keeping the terrible secret.

Brownie was waiting at the backdoor for them. He didn't need a bridle or a hackamore anymore, but let the children climb up to carry them to the bus. The autumn morning was clear and the chill in the air caused Kay to secure the top button of her coat. She let Charlie ride in front today and when they left the yard, Kay turned and looked back to the house. She could visualize her mother lying on the floor with father kneeling beside her. This is the image that she started out her day with, and the image stayed with her throughout it.

It was late afternoon when Mr. Collins dropped the children at the drive. Brownie was there to meet them. They didn't ride him to the house but walked quietly along with him. As they got closer they saw Aunt Gertie at the backdoor. She was a familiar sight as she had come so often during the summer to prepare supper for the family. Today she greeted the children ushering them into the kitchen where she had baked a batch of chocolate cookies. The house smelled like fresh melted chocolate and the kitchen was warm from baking. Gertie took Kay and Charlie's jackets and hung them up.

Kay was searching for any sounds in the house that might resemble last night's, but it seemed as if it held an emptiness, one where there was something physical for your whole life only to be missing, like an organ had been removed from one's body. She began to walk into the living room to pass by Mother's bedroom. The bedroom door was wide open. She went to it and walked a little ways into the room. The bed was tidy and made properly. The drapes were pulled back to let the light in, and she saw that her mother was no where to be seen.

She caught her breath and then she felt Aunt Gertie's hand on her shoulder. "It's alright Kay. Your mother is in the hospital." She said this with saddened resolve, but she tried very hard to be strong for her niece. Kay blurted out, "Mother in the hospital, which hospital, where?" Aunt Gertie told her that her father would be returning soon and that he would tell her everything when he got home. Kay's heart held her chest like lead and she turned away from Gertie and walked out the back door. She ran to Brownie where he stood as if waiting for her out by the swing tree. She ran up to him and cried out, "Oh Brownie, my Brownie, Mother is gone, Mother is gone…she's gone." She sobbed into his neck and he dropped his head almost to the ground so she could get a better hold.

Father did return with Father Davis, the family priest. Pat Davis was a huge man with a jolly face and a thick head of steel-gray hair. He was a loving prayerful pastor. He always tousled the children's heads and made light jokes with them when they left the church at the end of the Sunday service, so when Kay saw him with her father she knew that his presence was meant to comfort somebody. She knew no matter what he would say, there would be no comforting her that day.

Father looked worn and beat. He and Fr. Davis saw Kay with Brownie. Father walked over to them and told her to come into the house. He took her hand and she followed him, with Fr. Davis coming behind. When they walked into the kitchen Gertie met them and rose from her chair as she and Charlie were talking quietly at the table while he was finishing his cookie.

Father asked them to come into the living-room. Gertie got up and gestured Charlie to get up and come with her. The somber group processed to the couch and chairs under the window and sat down. It was Fr. Davis who began. He told the children that earlier that morning after Dr. Whitney left he, father, and Aunt Gertie took their mother to the hospital where she would go through some tests. "Your mother is very sick, and the doctor needs to find out exactly what is wrong." Now I heard that Kay was a big help to her father last night and I just want to say to you Kay how much I admire what you did for your father, and your mother." Then Charles spoke, "Kay and Charlie, your mother will be gone for awhile and I don't want you to worry. We are a family and Aunt Gertie will be here as she has for most of the summer, to help us after school and in the evening before bedtime." We will pray for Mother to get better so that she can come home.

After the talk in the living-room Aunt Gertie told us that supper would be ready in an hour so Father had an hour for chores. Gertie invited Fr. Davis to eat with them, but he declined telling her he appreciated it but thought he would drop by the hospital on the way back to the rectory. He got up to leave, patted the children on their heads, shook Aunt Gertie's hand and walked out the back door with Father close behind. They talked as father walked him to his car then he turned when Fr. Davis drove away and headed for the milking barn.

Kay could never know what happened in the milking barn but when Father came back into the house to wash up, his eyes were swollen. That night after father tucked the children into bed Kay fell asleep during her prayer. She kept saying over and over "Dear God, help Mama, help Mama. Dear God, please help Mama, please help Mama. Bring her home!" Her tears wet her pillow and where her hair lay out on the case it too became damp.

Whether God answered Kay's prayers she would never know if He helped her. Mother never returned to the house, to the children. This is where her faith wavered to be discarded eventually as Father never wanted to talk about their mother, but kept on with the daily chores of life giving all that he had to Kay and Charlie and the farm. The children only knew that their mother was "in the hospital" somewhere and whenever they rode Brownie down the road past Manteno State Hospital, only a mile or so down the road to the left of the drive, Kay wondered if she might be there.

Then it began happening at night. When it was truly dark Brownie would quietly unlatch his paddock door and walk silently past the house and down the road toward town. When he arrived at the Hospital he went down the road at the rear of the big building turned either right or left past the large H buildings. Each one had a name and there were so many, but for nights on end he would go to each one and peer into the windows that were lined down each side of the long part of the H. He could see many white covered beds with people in them sleeping. There were so many on each side of the H that it appeared that they were only a foot a part

124

from the other at all sides. If he could count he would find that perhaps fifty or more beds sat so close that one could barely walk between. In the rows of white sheets he pressed his face against the window to see if he could see mother's long flaxen hair sticking above the covers.

He spent many nights searching until one night when it was almost morning and the stars were paling in the sky he found her. She was lying facing him in the second row closest to the window about half way down. He recognized her face in its serenity; she looked like Kay. At this discovery, this is where Brownie came every night to keep watch over Mother Maude. If one happened down the road at midnight they would see a dark brown horse standing guard along the building.

He was certain that she would call him to take her home when it was time.

HEALING MOTHER OF PNEUMONIA:

AN ACCOUNT

Dedicated to my sister Margaret and
our journey to heal our mother.

One

LET'S rock around the clock tonight!! Let's rock, rock, rock 'till broad daylight... Sing it SISTER!! The oldies radio station boomed as the summer heat rushed through the rolled down windows. Margie's baseball cap held on to her white hair for dear life. I-90 was packed with afternoon commuters and our up-roarous singing at the top of our lungs was muted by the wind. Animated from road trip lust we sped across

America on what we know now was our mythic journey to heal our mother.

My sister Margie and I crossed the Missouri River at Dacoma, South Dakota earlier that morning and now the Mississippi River lay below us as we skirted Lacrosse, Wisconsin on our way to Watertown. It was mid-June. A cold spring hung around that year in the Pacific Northwest and the Northern Plains, and early wild perennials were just beginning to bloom. I had driven all night from Bellingham, Washington to Kalispell, Montana to pick Marg up. Just outside Sandpoint, Idaho at around two a.m. I took a pit stop in someone's field. I got out of the car which had the heater blasting, and from this warm cocoon I stepped into frigid air. I hurried my way to the edge of the field, and hunkered down against cold dewy grass. A chill shook me as I looked up into the heavens. I'd forgotten what the stars looked like. The moon was coming dark and the road was silent as a grove of thick cedars at midnight. There I squatted, cold and marveling in my homesickness for Montana and memories of this wild country.

I had driven for hours when the pale light of morning began to infiltrate the perfect starry night. As the last constellations stole across the sky to the west I was paralleling McGregor Lake. I was just coming into Kalispell when the sun peeked over the Mission Mountains. It promised to be an exemplary day; one Montanan's had waited a whole year for.

Marg was ready with her bags packed and a full travel cup brim-filled with coffee. We wasted no time getting on the road. I used the bathroom, washed my face, filled up a jug of coffee, said goodbye to her husband Jim and we hit the road, east. Margie took the wheel, as I had driven all night. We were armed with our medicine chest for Mom, oysters from Chuckanut Bay, massage oils, and our book <u>Women Who Run with the Wolves</u>. Our single most purpose was to heal our mother. Her pneumonia was hanging on as stubbornly as mold on blue cheese, and I knew I must go to her when I spoke with her on the phone and she said, come. Our mother wasn't someone who asked her daughters to travel over half of the United States because of a head cold. This was scary, and in her voice was weakness and need, something we weren't used to.

Marg, like all Montanans, has a feel for fast driving, speeding if you will. But what's the point in not speeding? No self-respective Montanan is going to drive the speed limit. For one thing it'd take forever to drive across the state, and for another who in god's name is ever going to corral a true-spirited Montanan? You might as well quit right here and now because it's about as unlikely as roping a Brahma at a rodeo. Marg was no different and soon we'd gone through Missoula, Butte, and were streaking through Bozeman Pass. The snow came down to around 1500 feet in the Crazy Woman and Absaroka Ranges. Even though the sun pelted us at soaring heights of around seventy-five those early spring perennials were just busting through the earth and finally showing their colors.

I slept for about a hundred miles.

We stopped in Hardin for hamburgers and that's when the gin came out. Our car bar was a liter diet Sprite container with about half the Sprite drunk. It was Marg's custom to pour the gin up to about "here," as she laid her finger three inches above the half-way mark. With a few swigs from the bottle we began our descent into Wyoming country. I woke up just before Billings and against the heat of day rolled our windows up so I could read our book, without losing my voice. Here is where "singing up the bones" emerged, and our mythic journey began in infancy.

You see it is La Loba, Wolf Woman who spoke to us. We were reading about her. She is a mythic creature who teaches women how to heal themselves. She says we must recapture our Wildness: our natural instincts. When we hear her and listen to her teachings she begins to sing a song over our bones, which causes our natural instinctive self to wake up. She gathers us to her using her soul-voice, and with each breath nudges us to sing up our bones and the bones of our mother. Without our Wildness we submit unknowingly to illness.

We heard her and listened and asked her to teach us. For we are wild and in our wildness we came to her as sisters of the same flesh and blood; of the same bones, from the same womb, only eighteen months apart. And now, we rush to our mother's side. What will you give us to take to her?

We would soon be leaving Montana, and I had vowed to pick a mullein plant for my mother's recovery, but it HAD to be from Montana. Just before we reached the border into Wyoming Marg pulled off the road. I went after a mullein that was off the road, down by the fence line. I took time out to ease myself from of the gin, so before I picked the plant I squatted down. As I looked up the embankment only five feet or so was the perfect skeleton of a calf. Some seasons ago it had just curled up and died. How long it had been there was undeterminable, but for some time there it lay undisturbed in its sweet instinctive curl. Right then, La Loba gave me sight. Here, Wildness gave us her bones. I stooped over the calf for a long time marveling at this epiphany. I knew then I was being offered the bones to take back to mother, for her healing.

I spoke to the animal's spirit and asked if I could take the jaw bones for an altar for my mother. As the afternoon breeze rustled the grasses, I instinctively knew that is exactly what I must do. I did the same with the mullein, made my way up the incline back to the car where Marg was waiting. In our minds we had just picked up our medicine. Our doctoring bag complete, we drove over the border into Wyoming.

Wyoming took only a few hours to burn through. We rolled along like a wind-pushed tumbleweed through that stretch between Sheridan and Gillette, only stopping for gas. On our approach to Spearfish country, just northwest of Rapid City, late afternoon's sun marked the turnoff to Devil's Tower. This is Wild country, wild and clear. Many bones could be collected here, as it is home to wolves, bear, deer, and badger. The wind played the grass like harp strings as we drove in silence. A world-between-worlds emerged in this place, a natural psychic wealth: more gifts for mother: meditation, prayer-making, creativity. We pooled our solitude and began our decent south into civilization.

It was 8:00 p.m. when we got our motel room in Rapid City. I don't remember when I slipped into sleep, but sometime during the night, in a corner of my dreams I heard thunder and rain. With my big sister lying next to me I felt safe like I did when we were children. Marg stirred first rousing me to wake up. We made no hesitation, no motel early morning TV. but quickly showered and dressed. When we opened the door the sky was barely light, and the storm that traveled through during the night left power lines dripping overhead. The air smelled sharply of fresh thunderstorm perfume; sunlight breached, like a happy whale on the horizon and bathed the undisturbed city in dawn.

We pulled out into the empty streets, found a truck stop for gas and coffee and broke through the city limits before six o'clock. We planned on driving South Dakota, Minnesota, and half of Wisconsin that day. As we drove out of town smells of flowered fields came up through the floor boards. I rolled down my window and hanging my head out inhaled with such fervor as to intoxicate every last nostril hair.

We envisioned La Loba loping beside us in her usual knowing way. We see her snort her breath into the wind as she plunges ahead through road mirages. She clears the path, all the while glancing back to see our expectant faces behind the car window.

We drove South Dakota making it to Sioux City by noon, then Minnesota in one fell swoop. The gin came out about cocktail time and we were feeling our mother now that Oconomowoc was within a two hour stretch. I was driving. Traffic picked up at Lacrosse and along with it pure adrenalin (not to mention the gin) shot into our pumping blood as we followed Eastbound I-90 toward Milwaukee. Our singing rifled the rushing air. We carried strong medicine from the Wild country to the tamer lands of the mid-west. Our Wildness ate up the road.

Two

She stood at the open door.

I went to her immediately feeling I must let her lean on me. She was bent forward, her chest sunk inwards where her body naturally formed a shelter around her lungs. The pneumonia clung like a spoiled child to its mother, only she was <u>my</u> mother, mine and Margie's and no one would keep her from us.

"Back to bed with you Mother" I spoke right up. She'd crawled out, we knew, to greet her daughters. No need for formalities. We chatted quietly with our brother Jon whose home Mom lived in. She had a small apartment in the rear, over the garage. My brother and his wife had given Mom the space during a time of homelessness after my dad died. She was often bouncing around from one daughter to the next, and after a few years of living with friends and staying for short visits with family needed a secure residence, after all she was almost eighty.

We walked her into her room where she sat down in the old rocker my father used to sit in while he read hour upon hour in his study. She had a modest room: a desk, a twin bed, a dresser, and two chairs were carefully arranged to save space. It might have been considered a nun's cell if it hadn't been for the large picture window that looked out to a very long backyard which ended at the shore of the Rock River. There, she watched wild ducks eat along the grass at the water's edge, often pruning the back yard for garden insects. The river rolled by under her meditative eye. Pictures of her eight children and numerous grandchildren stood on the dresser and adorned the wall. Familiar family relics assured us of our lineage: this lifetime: a Sterling.

I brought the mullein plant in from the car. I'd turned it upside down (as upside down as I could get it) in the trunk, with its roots still attached. In her weak attempt to visit mom soon tired while our robust energy filled the room and starting at her feet crept up her legs and encircled her entire body as we excitingly took over. I put that mullein right to work making a strong tea. "This is a Montana mullein Mom, it helps with upper-respiratory infections, and beings that it's from Montana believe me it'll heal you much quicker. She coughed a wretched hurtful cough which cued my swift move for the kitchen. A few bottles of Echinacea tincture were drawn from my bag. I knew she was on some heavy-duty antibiotics, but this natural herb couldn't hurt, not with Marg and me on the prescribing end, now.

We did visit with Mom as she sipped her tea and we unloaded our things taking turns bringing them in from the car. Soon after we completed our-getting-settled-tasks we tucked her in for the night. I had her roll on her stomach and massaged her back. I remember telling her what beautiful skin she had. How tight and youthful it looked, almost as smooth and supple as Claudette Colbert's, in her prime. The first night we were each given a bed far-distanced from mother's room and being so far from her felt as insecure as putting your sick baby in a room across the house from you. It just didn't make sense to us. It took us two nights to figure out we didn't feel good about it. The urgency of laying road down quick, through four states, was kinetic; a dose of it couldn't be withheld from mother. We decided then and there we would sleep in her room.

Jon directed us to the basement where he had a twin bed mattress in storage. Margie and I found it and hauled it upstairs and laid it on the floor right next to mom's bed. During those first two days Marg busied herself with making chiropractic appointments and rounding up any item Mom might need for alternative medicine: vitamin C (in large doses), all kinds of immune system builders, massage, and tea, tea, tea!

We spent much of our time meeting doctor appointments, rubbing Tiger Balm on Mom's chest, and expanding her field of energy by giving long drawn out Power Hugs. It's amazing what a Power Hug can do for healing. With Mother standing in the center, me to her back, Marg to her front, we sandwiched her between us, then together Marg and I would wrap our arms around her and hold on for dear life. Power hugs were big medicine.

La Loba says the symbol of seed and bone is much alike. If one has the original part it is the key to life, for *...havoc can be repaired, devastations can be resown, fields can be rested, hard seed can be soaked to soften it, to help it break open and thrive. To have the key means to dance with life, dance with death, dance into life again.*

At night, when it was time to sleep, Marg and I laid down on that single bed mattress. In the old days we would have an imaginary line drawn between us and woe to the guy who crossed over it. But, now thirty years later her presence honored me, and in her tiredness I offered to give her a rub. We could hear Mother's soft snoring which relaxed our efforts, and I had Marg turn away from me so I could reach her back, shoulders, and neck. I guess a great privilege in life is to massage someone to sleep. In it there is complete trust and comfort.

Stories are medicine.

They have such power; they do not require that we do, be, act anything--we need only listen. Stories are medicine.

"It's true Mom, these are the jawbones of the calf I found, or it found me." I re-lived the story of finding the calf skeleton. Maybe it didn't seem like much, but both Marg and I were believers now, believers that one can create a whole being from bones, which means something has died and is brought back to life by "singing up the bones." The story Clarissa Pinkola Estes told us about Wolf Woman, or Bone Woman, spoke to our inner souls just as clearly as the story of Jesus raising Lazarus from the dead. All one needs to do is find the bones, the beginning pieces, collect all of them, until there is a complete skeleton, then begin to sing and with your song visualize the flesh finding its way back onto the bones: sinews, muscle, organs, skin, and hair. Sing into it like the Holy Spirit breathes the breath of life into a seemingly dead soul, activating its indestructible life. This is not easy work. It is deep work and takes much prayer, singing, dancing, and instinct to create it. Our faith was sure-footed.

We read stories to her. I read my writing. She listened and her strength began to return. She sat up longer hours with us and as the days progressed into the week a marked change was seen in her vitality. By mid-week Margie and I knew she was getting better. We had only a few days left before we had to leave for home. Feeling certain of our mother's healing we began to prepare ourselves for our leave.

As I said earlier, the moon was coming dark. A dark moon ritual, before we left would act as cohesion to our united effort of boosting white blood cells and the immune system in our mother. Little did we know our suggestion to her to celebrate this ritual would be welcomed. Our sister Beth, who lived only fifteen minutes away wanted very much to be a part of the ritual, so we planned it, the night of the dark moon. We had much preparation to do.

Three

Today near eventide I did lead
the girl who has no seeing
a little way into the forest
where it was darkness and shadows were.
I led her toward a shadow
that was coming our way.
It did touch her cheeks
with its velvety fingers.
And now she too
does have likings for shadows.
And her fear that was is gone.

All day Marg and Beth were gone at the Mall. It was the night for the Dark Moon Ritual, and Marg wanted to get something for all of us. I had no idea what was taking them so long, but when they finally arrived they were all excited about the glorious beads they found for making "power" necklaces. It was Marg's idea and she had tediously picked over hundreds of beads. They had to be perfect, fitting for each individual design, for each person. When she showed me my necklace I was exhilarated. She'd chosen one jade-colored glass drop bead for the center with two cut black glass beads flanking it. The next beads on both sides were bone, above those crude light green and then, a brick-red round bead. All this was strung on a thin piece of leather. When I took it from her it fell, just so, into my hand. The long jade bead couched itself directly in my palm just about life-line position. It was startlingly smooth and cool. It's energy steady and vibrating. I wondered if she knew green was the color for healing, but guessed it didn't matter. She knew.

A Dark Moon Ritual is always performed at the dark of the moon. Here La Loba tells us how to recover parts of ourselves that are sick or lost, painful or self-destructive. She says the work is best done "in the shadows." This night as the moon goes dark we shall enter the shadows and search our darkened souls for that which makes my mother sick, and our own loss, transforming it in darkness. La Loba says we must use our "soul-voice."

We must say on our breath the truth of one's power and one's need, to breathe soul over the thing that is ailing or in need of restoration. This is done by descending into the deepest mood of great love and feeling, till one's desire for relationship with the wildish Self overflows, then to speak one's soul from that frame of mind. That is singing over the bones.

We prepared my mother's room for the ritual. An altar was made from a small table she had. We laid down a lovely scarf as altar cloth and each person placed something on the altar that symbolized spiritual power: my mother's crucifix, stones, flowers, the jaw bones of the calf, the power necklaces. It was time to begin. The doors were closed, the evening was waxing and darkness spread first from the corners of the room out. We, in its direct line sat around our altar: Mother, Margaret, Beth, and I. We placed representative objects at the four corners of the altar. Mother sat at the North symbolically representing the earth, Margaret sat at the East which is air, Beth sat at the South, fire, and I at the West, which is water. Each direction had a candle. It was our duty to create sacred space by beginning in the East. Margaret lit her candle and called upon the powers of the East to come and be with us. The wisdom of sunrise; the life-giving oxygen we breathe, and the wind under a bird's wing; Beth called upon the power of Fire with it's properties to purify; its warmth; its light; I lit the candle for the West asking the power of water with its oceans, lakes, rivers, and gentle rains to come to us and aid us in our healing and restoration; my mother called upon God, in Jesus name, Amen. She lit her candle and we all settled into each other's eyes and began to breathe as if to sing up the bones.

The idea for this ritual is to evaluate in yourself what you want or need to be healed, restored, or transformed. What is in the darkness can, and must, be brought out. To do this we wrote down that which we wanted healed, restored, or transformed on a piece of paper. We each had a black candle that would be lit when we read outloud our secret writing about ourselves. We began with Beth. Her personal plague of doubt and fear were identified and she set her paper on fire. As the smoke circled upward we imaged her shadowy nature going with it. I relinquished old fears and habits, then burned my paper in the black candle's flame. Mother asked, as she would at a prayer meeting, for God to enter each of us, and to bless us, and to heal her of her pneumonia. She thanked Jesus and the Holy Spirit then named her malaise: a surprising admittance, my father, as her source of illness. She burned her paper and sat stone-faced.

It was Margaret who was ignited by a spirit, so deep, so longing that as she began to read she began to sob about this Power that she had, it was too much power for her to handle. It expected too much and she couldn't deliver it right, she was always blowing it, always losing friends over it, but she had something so vast she didn't know how to handle it. She sobbed and sobbed and Mother began praying in tongues and we wanted to comfort her, but couldn't. Margaret's soul wrestled with this pain at such levels only the Spirit could understand. There was much struggle for composure. As I think back on this experience I realize this was a foreshadowing, a grip with Soul that is yet to be brought to fruition. When the soul-seizure passed, with our encouragement and love to support her she burned her paper in her candle's blaze and sent this declaration of pain and confusion into the East's air. There we sat silent, reverently wrung dry for a few moments before we took our white candles to light them with our visions of transformation.

Night had drawn itself up tight against the big picture window. The altar candles compassionately flooded our faces taking with it any wrinkled imperfections. From my chair in the west I waited silently and surveyed the altar one more time. Those jawbones, propped up against a sacred rock, shone in the candlelight, bleached and smooth. The jaw held a perfect row of baby teeth burrowed in, root-deep. I imagined these jaws living, with the ability to nibble on young shoots of prairie grass and suck the teats of its mother's bag. In death there was life. I saw it as I stared transfixed on the altar in candle light.

"I want my shadow to be replaced with confidence and self-belief," Beth said as she lit her white candle. She placed the votive in front of her and let it burn. I lit my candle, the whole time searching for what I really wanted to replace my fears, my abandonment from times past with. Was it courage or forgiveness? What?

La Loba tells us to not be afraid, for she watches us from her storeroom of skeletons, the ones she is bringing back to life. I hear her singing as she woos back the "dead and dismembered aspects of ourselves:" our Death Mother, our Creation Mother. Understanding strikes through instinct, and mine became keen and cunning. "Give me back to my Self, forgive me, help me to forgive and give me courage."

Margaret called upon her transformation like the priestess she is, lighting her candle with composure and with an attitude of habit as if she'd been lighting the altar candles every day of her life. She relinquished what had happened only moments ago into the candle's flame.

It was Mother's turn to be transformed.

"He's in me. He's right here, putting her fist against her chest. I need him out." She was asking for our help. This wasn't like mother for she had always led others to their healing, a spiritual leader they called her, but don't spiritual leaders need tending? In the quickness of breath in & breath out, her motherness changed, and there she was transformed, for we were no longer her little girls, but her spiritual equals. We all crossed over, through and into each other as we swam through that passage. This was my mother's triumph, her daughters knew well the Spirit.

It was these moments we received our instinct, once again, so noticeably to each other we all knew what to do, lead, follow, lead. My father had died almost eight years ago, and his ability to love was so limited its absence in my mother's life chipped away at her soul. Pneumonia was an emotional disease for mother, and we could see her breath lay backwards as she guarded it tight and painful like a tree growing around a nail.

La Loba knows about building skeletons. She knows forgiveness is mortar. Without it our bodies begin to fray like weak cloth. Eight years had passed since his death, and yet, he still hung onto her; he, the child clinging to its mother.

For eight years she had distanced herself from him, for he was secure beneath the big tree at Nashotah Cemetery. We had all been there, each piling a shovel-full of dirt over his ashes. Mother now free, her memories separated between past and present. She did something La Loba says to do; she detached from the loss of being loved. She set about building a new life, a free life. It was never like her to dwell on bitterness, but to let go of the pain. Jesus' example to "forgive them for they know not what they do" was as real to her as the tightening in her chest. She wanted to forgive him; she knew she must, but the time wasn't yet. It was her time to let go and run, run wild, and that's exactly what she did.

The dark moon offered no forgiveness ritual, but something delicately potent. Instinctually, we went to mother forming a crescent around her. Margaret put her hand on Mother's back, Beth put her hand on Margaret's back, and I put my hand on Beth's back. We knew exactly what to do, even though we'd never done it before. We saw our father nestled like a baby against our mother's lungs. He was innocent and precious. I said, Marg take him from her, and she did, then she handed him to Beth, and she in turn handed him to me. I released him back to the Creator, into the arms of his loving Father and Mother.

La Loba knows *one of the most profound forms of forgiveness is to give compassionate aid to the offending person in one form or another...respond from a stance of mercy. Forgiveness is an act of creation (whether) forgiven now, then or the next time...*we have many chances to forgive, in part, or wholly. It is all apart of the process. We understood what Jesus meant when he said to "forgive seven times seventy."

Beth handed mother a match to light her white candle. She did, and we sat back down around the altar. The shadows in the room danced in the light of our candles. Quietly, we began to unwind time by closing the sacred circle. First mother, thanking God and Jesus and the Holy Spirit, then me, blessing the waters of the West and letting them go, then Beth, blowing her altar candle out, dismissed the power of the South, and last, Margaret releasing the power of the East to return, or stay, whichever it wanted. Like acolytes, we doused the altar's flames and began to move about in the darkened room to turn on the lights.

There's never a lot to say after something like this. In all honesty I can't remember how or when we parted and said goodnight. I do remember the change in Mother. She was much stronger, and I mean so much that she, in no way, resembled that bent person we met at the door almost a week ago. She was our mother again: able, staunch, and sure.

She rose before us the next morning. I could smell coffee aromatherapy coming from the kitchen. Marg was stirring, and for a brief moment I pretended Mom would come into the bedroom, like she did when we were young girls, and even until we were young women, in our teens. She used to climb the stairs from the second to the third floor on most mornings to wake us. I recall it was an embarrassment when we were older because she inevitably always wanted to nuzzle, and I used to get perturbed thinking geez, she's got a baby downstairs, but oh, now how I love that about her.

That morning was our final morning to spend with mother. Tomorrow we would be driving out of Wisconsin to head west, toward home. The weather had turned hot and muggy, and it reminded me of full-on summer, with lighting bugs and the whole works.

We didn't know it then, but mother's wildish nature had withered into sickness, and we, her daughters heard her howl from four states away. Our instincts were right, and the time for us to act had come. Mother was healed now and it was time to go home.

Four

What is homing? It is the instinct to return, to go to the place we remember."

Clarissa

Pinkola Estes

We'd picked up La Loba just crossing the Montana/Wyoming line on our trip to the mid-west. She left her duties there to come with us. Our mother's call was high on the wind and through the sweeping valleys of western Montana did she pick up her cry. We traveled with her from that gully along the highway where I first found the calf skeleton, and now, her work complete she disappeared without so much as a tail wave. I

143

suspect another skeleton was stirring back in her cave, and she needed to continue singing over it's bones.

Margie and I were fledglings when it came to accepting our Wild force; as mid-age women we'd escaped from the dangers and pitfalls of our innocent youth, and now were being made ready for our Wild work. We didn't know what was yet to come in our lives, but at that moment were as wild as any wild animal living on the High Prairie. Embracing our healing with mother we made ready for the journey home. I wore my power necklace and with our new stock of gin we packed the car and with kisses flying left Jon's block with our windows rolled down to ward off the humidity and heat.

We decided to take a diversion home. We wanted to go back to our childhood home in Chadron, Nebraska. It'd been twenty years since I'd been back, and I remembered the last time I was there was in the middle of the Lakota Sioux Indian wars on the U.S. Government in 1973. Chadron was stock full of U.S. Marshals, and the small town was over-run with FBI agents and State and County law-enforcement agencies. Russell Means and his band of "renegades" had finally had it with corrupted Indian agents and, between a rock and hard place, fought back killing two FBI agents. All hell broke loose, a town under siege. Stopping for gas I overheard someone say the town was going to be burned down! It ended with great injury to the Sioux at Pine Ridge Reservation.

This was the quiet unassuming ranching community where Marg and I had spent eight years of our childhood. Our father had a parish there, he, an Episcopal priest. The small town of Chadron, in my estimation was unscorned by life. Its intimate lifestyle, where everybody knew everybody, played its role in the '50s. We were protected there and played, acting out our little dramas and fantasies, daily on the corner of Bordeaux Street. Everyone knew the priest, his wife and six little girls. Hot dry summers saw four or five little girls dressed in summer gingham dresses strolling doll-buggies, or swimsuit clad, running through the hose.

The front porch of the rectory was maybe fifteen feet from the front door of the church. That line between home and church was not well defined. Our play spilled into the nave. We were often found playing hide and seek in the pews or acting out a dramatic wedding with the neighborhood kids. Our oldest sister Mary, and Margie, were promoters of fun and wars. There were times of scratching, biting and scaring the bejesus out of each other, but mostly, we took turns and the little ones gave in to the older sisters. The church sanctuary held our worship, our play, and sometimes our tantrums. A very lively place!

The flowerbeds around the stone church were filled with red salvia and placed in front of them was a big sign that read GRACE CHURCH EPISCOPAL. Many of our pictures were taken in front of that sign: little girls, like corn, all in a row. "C" hill was this monstrous hill which Chadron was built against. It had a few sparse Ponderosa pines and Juniper growing sporadically about and there were trails up it, but it was way out of our territory. Besides, it was hotter than a mighty south wind on the prairie in the summertime.

We had numerous outings: Chadron State Park, picnics and church at Holly. Holly, Nebraska never was on a map. I recall from childhood, and a few pictures, there was only a stark white church with a matching outhouse out in the middle of the prairie. Laura Ingalls Wilder might've described a place like Holly in her book <u>Little House on the Prairie</u>.

A handful of saints worshiped there when my father came for services. The land, covered with tall grasses, waved endlessly in ocean tides of timothy, rye, and wild oats. The church was really only a shell for the Almighty with crude pews and little windows of clear glass. My mother would unload the picnic from the car then spread out a blanket on the open hillside. There were no trees, no shade. Even when it was blistery hot a prairie wind brought relief. My sister's and the other kids would run about pretending to be Roy Rodgers and Dale Evans; I was always a horse, usually Trigger or Hop-a-long Cassidy's, Topper. We explored what there was to explore, which left a lot up to the imagination.

One Sunday, someone found a bull-snake under the foundation of the church. It sought refuge from the heat there, but hadn't contended on the Sunday worshippers to disturb its retreat. From around the church we heard "Come'ere!! Quick!!! Some lad had looked under the church and there it was ten feet long and thicker than a drain pipe. I came around the corner of the building just in time to see him pulling on it with a stick he'd found. I stopped dead in my tracks, withdrawing in horror at its great immensity. My dad kept saying it wasn't poisonous, but poison wasn't exactly what I was thinking of, more like being swallowed alive. Eventually, the boy was told to leave it alone and it crawled way back under the foundation, out of reach. That was the biggest event that ever took place at Holly, and probably for a long, long time in my young life.

Often our parents would take us over the roller-coaster hills to Hot Springs, South Dakota for a dip in the monolithic Evans plunge. It was about forty-five miles away. We'd pass the turnoff road to Pine Ridge, a place our father had affiliations with, but that's another story. It was high prairie, and when I say high prairie I remember its clear air and miles upon miles of fifteen-hand horse-high grasses. Buffalo roamed free and wild and we could always count on their herds being along the roadside; we often had to wait for them to cross the road: bulls, red-eyed in the heat and the cows kicking up dust while their calves impatiently ran beside them trying to catch up long enough to nurse.

Our neighborhood was only a few blocks from downtown, but downtown might as well've been miles away. It was "down there," if we were ever asked. Our world was the block, and sometimes under supervision we got to go to the swimming pool, or even to "Newsy Nook," the local magazine and newspaper store. There we'd charge in with our nickel for penny candy and load up for the long three block walk home. We frequented the movie house on Saturdays for the matinee. It cost a dime to get in and a dime for popcorn. The house was usually packed, and the first films rolled were Newsreels. Black and white film with loud announcers who annunciated every sentence with headline propensity imprinted on our memories what reparation of war meant. President Eisenhower was running for office again, with Mamie at his side in her weird buster-brown bangs. Jackie Robinson was breaking records in baseball and bazaar human interest stories such as live cats worn as stoles, raced across the screen. Newsreels were kind of entertaining, but we lived for the weekly serial. Tarzan was the serial of the year with Lex Barker flexing his muscles. He was competition for Johnny Weissmuller that was for sure. His jungle call brought on stampeding elephants and screeching monkeys and apes. He could swing vines real good too. The snakes were powerful in the Congo, and we sat on the edge of our seats when Tarzan tangled with a twenty foot an Anaconda in the water (I could have sworn the bull snake at Holly was an Anaconda). Lex Barker was tough, like Fess Parker, and we lived for Saturdays to see if he'd survived his last perilous predicament. This was Chadron, our world.

Everyone knew us. The seasons passed for eight years, but summer was the time we remembered the best. This trip was long in coming; it was summer, almost the 4th of July, and oh, the celebrations on the 4th: rodeos, fireworks, picnics, and parades, and this year Margie and I would be there for all of it.

Five

We expected a heat-wave with soaring temperatures and high humidity, but as we crossed the Wisconsin/Illinois border there was something different in the wind. We'd pictured the first part of the trip as a potential hell-hole and would bypass Chicago just past the border at Beloit. Our plan was to drive south to Rochelle taking Highway 88 to Rock Falls, which was just a stick's throw across the Rock River to Sterling and Dixon country. Sterling, Illinois was named after our great, great Grandfather James Sterling. Our dad had been born and raised in Dixon where he and Ronald Reagan and Helen Meyers had graduated in the same class in high school. Our grandfather, dad's dad, was a pharmacist for Walgreen-Sterling pharmacy, and he and Uncle Bob worked together in the family business. Almost all the Sterling's never left the mid-west except for our family, and I think it was because of my father's wildness.

Marg and I drove along making fast paces. We didn't stop in Sterling country, but took it in as we whizzed by. There was a low-lying cloud layer, more like pollution than clouds, and in my imagination I thought I could smell the scent of prairie air just over the next hill. Our connections were to more wild country, vast and bigger than all get out on a clear day.

Somehow, our straight-ahead-line of driving got confused. Our instincts were muddled as we looked down the unfamiliar highway under that flat gray sky. I was a bit disappointed wanting the searing heat of a humid mid-west day, to tell stories about when we got home, of the overbearing hardship of passing through this unattractive country. The temperature hadn't budged since we'd left Wisconsin, but rather stingy, like slough-mud puddled with stagnant water, hung limply like clothes drying on a line on a windless day.

How we missed the highway to Moline was beyond us. We couldn't figure it. Where had we made the wrong turn? We questioned that one, but for some reason weren't interested in turning around and hunting and pecking our way back to a civilized way to cross Iowa. We couldn't imagine not crossing Iowa on the freeway, and had planned to speed through it, not looking right or left, but on a tailwind, hopefully, to make it through the state in only a few short hours. This didn't turn out to be the case at all.

It must have happened around Sterling country, but we ended up in a little town called Clinton, just north of Moline. Now Clinton is where Highways 30, 67, and something else converge. We took the something else highway which ended up taking us smack across the middle of the state, miles away from the one freeway that goes through Iowa. Instead of dumping out at Omaha we would go at right angles all the way to Sioux City. A slight detour in our detour, but remember La Loba was no longer leading us.

We jumped across the Mississippi River at Clinton and best to my knowledge nothing looked any different than any other day in Clinton, Iowa. The weather was still holding dull, like an inversion of soily air; the heat still window-down hot. We found Highway 30 again, a strip of two-lane freeway heading north to Waterloo. We might as well travel north to get across because we'd have to get north to get on target for Chadron, which was clean at the other end of Nebraska. Why not get in line now?

Maybe they'd changed the map since we looked at it last, but who would have thought, from looking at a map of Iowa, when the thick blue line ran out and the skinny red line started would be the beginning of one slow, right-angle, pig-stinking, boring ride. Margie was driving, and I just had to sit there looking at one pig farm after another. At fifty-five miles per hour you get to see a lot of pig farms, and the stink of those pigs was powerful. We'd be driving along holding our noses and just when we thought we were safe to let go the thinning pig smell would come on hard and thick. Tires through a foot of mud might describe it, but the mud ain't mud, if you know what I mean? With Iowa boredom bearing down on us, and the wicked smell of grunt there was only one thing left to do, drink.

Out came the gin. Iowa made us do it. Better to be killed drinking than dying of boredom. Since I wasn't at the wheel I imbibed the heaviest. Before twenty miles had gone by I was pretty stinken' drunk. I didn't complain about the "pig inversion" anymore, but got lively in my liquor. Margie was hooked by road ease. The miles turned into stories and before long we thought everything was hilarious. We pretended like the cops in Iowa didn't pull over traffic offenders, they sniped 'em from overhanging tree branches, or from behind tall corn. We knew they disguised their police cars to look like hay trucks, only to pursue speeding motorists with hay flying out from behind in a vortex while they shot guns from their windows. I even saw a sign that said "Drunk Driving Laws Harshly Enforced. We Shoot Drunks!" I know it was there, Margie says she saw it too.

Now, I'm sorry to talk that way about Iowa, but for god's sake, a million pig farms, and whoever laid out the state did it a hundred and fifty years ago when you traveled from one farm to the next, in a day. Before we knew it we were making a left turn, not curve, at Fern, then a left and a jog at Parkersburg, then over to Austinville where you turned left, then right again, and all this in about seven miles. Need I say more? This was the next two hundred miles.

The gin wore off as we settled into our plight, commenting on the wilderness in middle-America. The isolation reminded me of logging communities back off the beaten track in Western

Montana. Or, living like my friend Kathy at the end of a seventeen mile dirt road out of Lame Deer, Montana. This was equal to it, but linear. Isolation caused by complete right angles, an ordered network of roads with abrupt corners, in short distances, about the length of a farmer's field. The town's looked the same, and the people too, like the picture in *The Family of Man*, (a book of photographic essays): hearty farm women with round faces and hair pulled back in '50's hairstyles whose capable arms were heftier than their husbands. They ate well and with purpose because the fruit of their labor didn't come easy. In this community of insiders I detected a life from the land set in a dye of straight lines like corn rows, homemade white bread, and marshmallow fruit salads. The one technical devise from the outside world were scores of satellite dishes. When passing through Rowan or Thor, or Eagle Grove almost every house had one. To say houses have chimneys is to say houses have satellite dishes, in Iowa.

We'd been playing Willie Nelson's "America" song for the last hundred miles. It was written for America's farmers during his Farm Aid days. Willie's crooning subdued our blood, and with the wind picking up a bit the haze of Iowa's low pressure cloud cover began to lift as we finally reached Sioux City.

Six

Now I could smell the sweet grasses of Nebraska!
The wind shifted shortly after we passed through Sioux City. An easterly began to blow sluicing dull clouds into fragments; they dispersed high into the

152

atmosphere bringing bright sunshine. Marg and I'd been on the road well into mid-day. After Iowa, it was as if a rodeo bronc-chute gate was opened and out we burst, a tailwind pushed us west.

Thunderheads lifted high on the horizon. In my relief to be out of Iowa I turned to Margie and said satisfyingly, "Well Marg, we're going home now. Mom's healing and now we go home to Chadron." Marg's expression shifted as she tucked her hair into her hat and she said out of the blue,

Kath, I didn't tell you this because, well, I just couldn't, but the ironic thing is that mom's old and she's healing, and I'm young and it might be me who's dying.

She was driving and between the crescendo of wind and open windows I didn't get what she was saying. Oh yeah, I said, that's a good one.

She told me she was going to pull over at the next stop. I said fine. So why'd you say that? I mean Iowa was bad, but, God you say it like you're serious.

"I am."

"What are you talking about?"

"I've got cancer. Ovarian cancer."

"Bullshit."

"It's true."

"Bullshit!! I call you."

"It's the truth. I just found out. I got a phone call with the test results just before we left."

"That's bullshit. If you even remotely thought you'd have cancer why would you go on this trip with me? The doctor's wouldn't let you."

"What can they do about it? I can do anything I want to. They don't have anything to say about it. What was I going to do just sit there and wait for test results? There was a good chance I wouldn't have cancer. I had to come on the trip with you Kathy. I couldn't stay home and just wait. What am I gonna do, get sympathy from Jimmy? Forget it. Mom needed me."

I sat staring at her, dumbfounded, then spoke under my breath, "But you've been fine...I mean, all this time on the road, at mom's. What the hell? What's wrong with you?"

"I started getting a pain in my side. They thought it was my appendix, but to tell the truth I've felt like shit since Christmas."

"...but you've never said one damn thing to me."

"I didn't feel like it. You, for one person should know my complaints. Hell I've been fatigued and exhausted half my damn life, so why should I go on complaining every time I turn around."

"So be a martyr..."

She found a side road and pulled the car up short peeling gravel from under the tires.

"Let's deal with this right now!"

My voice lifted, "I've got to get you back! What are we taking this diversion to Chadron for? You have to get back, NOW. We wasted all that time in Iowa. Jesus we could've been wandering around Iowa for a week, lost in pig crap!"

"Quit being mad Kathy! Just stop it!"

"You lied to me all this time. I thought we were close. You can't even tell me?"

"I didn't lie to you. What was I going to do just break down with the news as we were leaving? Mom's not completely well yet."

"So, you didn't tell her either?"

"How could I? She's sick!"

"This can't be happening," my voice faltered "Fuck, cancer..."

My eyes settled stunned on the edge of the grassy field. Fear was lost to grief.

I started crying and hugging her, and she resisted the truth and held firm her tears as the wind rushed in my ears and my tears fell hot and torrid upon her collar. I said through short sobs.

"I don't want to lose you. None of us could lose you Marg. Nobody in our family has cancer, why you?"

She just sat there staring into the field. She seemed to be catching a wave on the bending grasses in the field. She rode it for awhile. Then she almost whispered.

"I'm not going to die."

Then I felt shame for breaking down. Where was my faith? I scanned the bending grass for any sight of La Loba, and in the wind I thought I heard her howl. I even said,

"Margie, did you hear something?"

She said, "No."

I shored up, like a boat pulled up on a beach.

"What's going to happen?"

"I'm scheduled for surgery when we get back, next week."

"So soon?"

The wind blew from my lungs blowing the feather on the rear view mirror.

Why my mind shot back to a sweater Margie had knitted for her daughter when she was a baby was a complete mystery. Then, I instantly remembered her bruised hip where the iron shot had left its blackened mark all those years ago after her second daughter Meghan had been born. These images flooded, in with others. The tightening in my throat was unbearable, but I said, rather mulling it over as I searched for the faith to believe it.

"You're strong Margie. I know you can beat this thing. We can beat it. Do what you have to with the doctors, anything they say, but we've got to believe you can be healed. This trip must be part of it. God, how could we have known? Don't worry. I'll do anything for you. I'm with you Marg. I mean, I'm really with you!!"

Margie would not give in to the thought she had cancer. She just kept sitting there as if helicoptering above the reality. Eventually, she reached over and laid her hand on my thigh.

"Let's hit the road, o.k.? You drive. It'll do well for me to just ride."

I pulled out onto the highway, as I pushed the accelerator, the landscape blurred by. The sun streamed on my arm and leg causing a pleasurable penetration. We settled dumbly into Nebraska.

My clutch foot resting on the dash eased the small of my back. It's unimaginable to travel this fast on ground. After awhile we tried singing along with Willie, but the wind was picking up to a ferocious force. The sun was still ducking in and out of scattered storm systems and hung in between clouds causing my arm and leg to redden up. I had to keep the window down. So did Margie because it was hot enough to make a sealed ride intolerable. Of course they were rolled all the way down leaving our shirts and hair flapping and flying raucously about.

We aren't wimps when it came to taking on a force, whether it's trouble, sickness, or birthing a baby alone at home (me); we're sisters with grit. Our hair got hung in the wind, snarled and whipped. I tied a scarf over my head and tied it tight at the back. My left ear was beginning to hurt because the whistling of the wind screamed, hammering on my eardrum. Still, we didn't roll up the windows. We didn't talk either, couldn't.

By the time we'd driven through Antelope County and were heading well into Holt we thought we'd best break for gas and potty. Marg filled up the tank while I washed the windows and stretched my legs. Putting one foot on the grill I bent my knee inwards flexing my low back muscles. Stretch-squat-backbend. It was her turn to pay for the gas, when we both heard talk about the Mississippi River flooding like hell, especially at Dubuque, Iowa. It was a catastrophe up there, and we had just crossed the Mississippi at Clinton just about sixty miles south from Dubuque. I didn't notice one thing different about that in-descript crossing, other than the fact we found ourselves in the wrong town on the wrong road.

It was real bad, a national disaster. Somehow, when we drove across the Iowa border we slipped through the veil into the Otherworld. They talk about this in Celtic lore: the thin mist or veil between the worlds. Now, as we made our way through Nebraska we found we missed some big part of life in the mid-west and we, just only hours ago, had been right in the middle of it.

The wind howled as if ten packs of wolves ran along side the car. The sky threatened rain and hail, and god knows what else, but it didn't come. The sun kept skirting the clouds and reigned on us. The openness of Nebraska began to move from flat lands into gentle rolling hills. It opened up in front of us and we sped along like wind through a whistle. We were tiring, but as we approached familiar territory, like the little town of Gordon we saw signs of the Fourth of July celebrations, which were only tomorrow away. Flags were out. In the midst of rodeo signs and July fourth banners, the early crack of ladyfingers could be heard in pockets around town. The air was filled with expectation of a day that was usually hot and dusty. Not this year though. The wind was proving cooler, even a bit chilly.

Margie and I began to relive our memories. We'd been to Gordon, and someone had the slide of some of the family standing in front of our station wagon somewhere in Gordon. It was hot because we were all sunburned and dressed in crop tops and shorts. There was this country, down-home air around us. Those slides contained many hot summer day portraits of hiking the Black Hills, swimming at Chadron State Park, and watching the Sioux Sun Dances up north.

Somehow, we'd passed through summer's heat and back into spring. The thunderheads, widespread across Nebraska earlier in the day, blew in some rain. We rode into Chadron around suppertime. The road had wet spots and the smell of a storm still lilted in the evening air. It was all so unfamiliar to me: the valley; the terrain of the lay of the land. We found our motel along the highway heading toward Hot Springs. It was on the edge of town, and our room was your typical double bed affair. Somehow it felt, to me, more than a strange motel room in a one horse town, but cozy and friendly, maybe even Chadron's finest. We unloaded our overnight bags, poured a gin and decided to head into Chadron to eat and get acquainted with our once sterling childhood home.

We drove around town, first. Downtown really hadn't changed that much. Newsynook was gone, and the theatre had been modernized. There were new businesses, but truthfully there wasn't a Wal-Mart impact in Chadron. The town was still pristine in its small town portrait. The streets were clean, and the big trees lined the neighborhood down by Dr. Kershawn's house. He used to have a parrot thirty years before, the parrot outliving him by half a century. Time hadn't progressed much. If people hadn't moved on or died little had changed, and rapturously enough from my child's eyes to my adult's eyes it seemed much the same.

We found Grace Church. The rectory had been torn down some years ago to build a parish hall. We'd heard it'd been done a while back so we weren't disappointed. Otherwise it was the same. Marg and I got out of the car and stood at the red fire hydrant on the corner. This was the best picture-shot for the church so we took turns taking pictures of each other. I swear, when we passed through the mists somewhere just out of Iowa, time was lost. It felt as if time passed unnoticed, in my psyche that is. Margie and I were little kids again, but we drank gin. Now, that's a powerful spell for sure because everything felt fresh and innocent. It would last for less than twelve hours.

We were hungry, and the light of day gradually lost itself into the western sky. Dark grays and sunless light stole across the valley and nestled in the draws up toward the high prairie. We found a ranchy restaurant, one with six things on a plate of ribs: potatoes, beans, salad, garlic toast, and a cinnamon apple slice. We diverted from gin and ordered a beer. Just as we were coming in the bar and grill two Indian men saw us and made a pass. We gingerly passed by them, not making eye contact and walked into the restaurant. They, perhaps, were the offspring of the Pine Ridge Indians who knew our father in the old days.

The waitress had lived in Chadron all her life, which were about two-thirds of our lives. She confirmed it hadn't changed much, and boy was she glad. She'd moved to Lincoln once, but made it back as fast as she could. We told her we'd lived here back in the '50's, and were making a pilgrimage back home. She was gabby, and entertained us for a few minutes until she heard her name called for an order, up and briefly left us to ourselves.

The bar and grill was dimly lit with red and white gingham table cloths and matching napkins. A recollection of what it means to be a westerner is stamped indelibly on the collective unconscious in gingham. Red and white checks, in cotton are culturally spread across restaurant tables all over the old west.

"Makes you feel right at home, huh?"

I said, "Yeah. It reminds me of anywhere in Montana": Helena, Bozeman, Butte, Livingston, Hamilton, Kalispell, or Thompson Falls, St. Regis, or West Yellowstone.

The waitress appeared with our beers, set them on the table, and said it might be awhile for food. We told her no hurry. The day's drive and events began to rest heavily against our bones. We sipped our beers and slumped a bit in our chairs. We hadn't talked about M's diagnosis since crossing into Nebraska. We'd passed collapsed barns along our way, remnants left broken from heavy snows long past. We rode silent letting Willie repeat, mile after mile, his melodious mantras.

Marg drew a light sip of her beer and said wistfully,

"Remember those early morning communions at Camp?"

Why she suddenly materialized communion at Camp Marshall was a surprise, but her very mention of it jostled my memory and just as suddenly as she thought it up and called me there I was standing in the rough cut log pews at the edge of Flathead Lake.

She talked about our summer we spent at the church camp. All ten of us in our family slept in an old boathouse which had a wooden floor built in. It had a huge swinging door on the lakeside. When that door was wide open we could sit on the edge of the floor and dangle our feet in the water. The wind would blow through the structure with a gusty force rustling the hanging bathing suits hung on nails to dry. If you climbed into your bunk and lay on your belly on top of your sleeping bag you could feel the wind blow over your back. We brushed our teeth with lake water and too often ended up in for a swim. How cold that water could get!

After devouring at least half our plate loads we settled up and drove back to the motel. Neither of us had much left to say.

We set Marg's alarm for real early and pulled up an extra blanket on the bed. When we tucked under the covers she turned her back to me to go to sleep. I reached out my hand and rested it gently on her hip. I whispered "I love you Margie". She said she loved me too. My mind jumped from thinking of comforting words to silent screams of prayer, then two or three sighs, and finally imaging my life force going from my heart through my arm and out my fingers into her hip, her belly, and into her heart. My last silent word was, "heal".

The Fourth of July arrived in a burst of sunlight. The sky was clear, but it was definitely cool. The brightness of the day had nothing to do with the holiday; it was because our homing began to seize us giving us a communion as clean and pure as we remembered it when we were children. We left the motel by 5:45 and drove straight to C Hill. It was Sunday. Marg and I bypassed the church with our eyes on that big whitewashed C. The sun shown on the dew and as it etched its way onto the Hill we parked the car in the college parking lot, found the trail and started our hike. Along the way the rose hips were just budding. We started picking gathering our precious jewels from this windswept hill.

With a holy reverie we hiked the trail picking, picking, picking. I'd seen hatbands made out of rosehip buds and saw how lovely they dried making it possible to keep them for years. I thought back on the trip out to Wisconsin how La Loba had sniffed us out at the border. We had to gather our medicine chest then, and now we were gathering the natural gardens of this fine high country. In those rosebuds lay the inevitable art of creation. We picked and sniffed and lay our faces into the breeze. In thanksgiving we decided to make a lei for mother: rosebuds from Chadron: a gift. We filled an old shoebox we'd gotten out of the trunk with the 'hip buds. It's dry in this country, and the Ponderosa pine was dwarfed from lack of rain and too much wind. Sparse bunch grass grew beside rocks, and the dryness of the place pushed the dust out from underneath our feet as we trekked the trail. We wandered and picked all over the face of C Hill.

Not until we'd had enough rosebuds and felt the first twinges of hunger did we separate ourselves from the hill. On our drive down into town we passed one more time by Grace Church. The eight o'clock worshippers were arriving for the service. We decided to go peek in the front doors of the church to see how it had changed. We were met by an older gentleman who was handing out bulletins. He was wonderfully friendly, so much we told him we used to live in Chadron when we were children. Grace Church had been our dad's church in the '50's. He said, "You mean Chandler Sterling is your dad?" We said, "Was our dad." He smiled as he took in the news of his passing. He said he was sorry to hear the news, but went on saying, "Well, your dad married me and my wife." How appropriate. Something's in Chadron don't change. He's still an usher after forty years.

He asked us if we were coming to the service. "No, we can't today. We have to be on the road within the hour," we lied. We did lie too. We had yet to drive out to Chadron State Park before we split for Montana. True, the minutes were ticking by, and our homing wasn't complete yet, but lying to the usher that Dad married at Grace Church was altogether unnecessary, except in a way that linked our distance from the institutional church as adults to our little girlness needing to tell a lie. Avoiding a church service had to happen at that time in our lives. We couldn't be tamed right then, not even for a forty-five minute communion service. We shook the man's hand and peeked into the church. If we'd stayed for church there's no telling what might've happened. Mother had heard Jesus speak to her from the giant cross one Lent in the sanctuary all those years ago. She was changed forever and having been an agnostic since she lost her mother to mental illness in her childhood, believed for the first time since she married my father and became a priest's wife.

As we walked through the vestibule the first verse of a familiar hymn escorted us out the door. The muffled organ sang sweetly, and the congregation began to sing the all to familiar hymn:

Beneath the cross of Jesus I fain would take my stand,
the shadow of a mighty rock within a weary land,
a home within the wilderness, a rest upon the way,
from the burning of the noontide heat and the burden of the day.

Before the second verse could lure us back we were getting into the car and driving out of town toward Chadron State Park. The park laid six, or so miles from town. The day continued in bright sunshine, and as we traveled the well-paved road everything seemed clean, almost flawless. When we got to the entrance of the park it didn't represent anything I'd remembered in the past. The shade from lovely foliage was imprinted on my mind. In times past we had to ford a creek that spilled over the road. It was supposed to do that because it never dried up throughout the year. It was one of those mixes where nature and human meet in harmony. The pleasure of driving through it with tires splashing water in every direction was only superseded by having the barefoot joy of running through the skimming water along the pavement. Little heads hung out the window as mother, or dad revved the car a little to make the splash bigger.

To Margie's and my great disappointment the creek had been rerouted, or the road, but nonetheless, the beauty of that simple pleasure had been eradicated at the park. To make matters worse the crotchety old swimming pool was absolutely gone. Where once it's huge concrete body laid, a pond'd been built. Oh, such a pool, like no other in the land, gone forever. I felt grieved as we talked about learning to swim in the shallow end where the deep end was separated by a rock wall. The water was dark as the bottom was gray, not brightly painted white, but crudely built. The concrete was beginning to crack up way back then and frogs weren't uncommon to swim with, but it was the water on a blistering summer day for a gaggle of little girls which made our lives in Chadron magic. Those two wonders of our world no longer existed.

The pond was alright, but in no way did it offer any enticement. The park was so clean. It was a State park, impeccably ruled, one could tell, the cabins for rent were freshly painted with green trim; all the garbage cans were painted the same color and the trails from the parking areas to the front porches were well tended and worn. Each of those little cabins had a screened-in front just like the old days. We could smell the pines and the dusty trails and could hear the mad leg-scratching of grasshoppers in the tall grasses. Between the memory moments and displacement in a perfect world we played out one last drama. Uncovering the garbage cans we threw all kinds of debris on the ground around them then took turns taking pictures standing beside our handiwork. We laughed our meanness out, picked up the trash, shoved it into the cans and drove out of Chadron State Park vowing to rent a cabin sometime.

The gnawing in our stomachs crescendo into a full blown symphony by the time we'd gotten back to town. We chose a friendly looking cafe with a lot of cars parked around it. It looked like the 4th of July was starting to percolate. Coffee should be hot, and we craved a cup. Upon entering the cafe there was a short line, mostly locals, and of course, the regulars all in their late sixties and seventies. The codgers lit up when we walked through the doors. Old men in three-way blue and white plaid shirts with shiny polyester western cut pants flashed smiles. "What are you two ladies up to this mornin'? Gitten' ready for the parade?" "Sorry, can't say we are. We're just passing through Chadron this morning." The hubbub of clattering dishes and tables shoved together to accommodate large groups of cowboy hatted guys and crispy white-bloused ladies embellished the dawn of the day's excitement. Eggs sunny-side up, or a short stack was yapped by waitresses to cooks, and the cackling of a bleached blond waitress with a large derriere rang the order-in bell. It would be a 4th to remember, in Chadron.

After our runny eggs and white toast we paid the bill, flirted with the old boys, saying our good-byes and teasing them about breaking the eight seconds on their bull rides at the rodeo then climbed into Pearl (my Toyota Tercel), and headed off into the mid-morning sunshine.

We'd done it, homed ourselves. We thought about La Loba because we'd done what we needed to do, go back to a place we remembered. I turned and looked down the road to Chadron's city limits as we pointed Pearl north. With a deep-longing sigh we geared up to charge back through the Mists to the awaiting road ahead.

Seven

Margie's mission to tear up the road knows no limits. She's a slave driver when it comes to dishing out miles and lays them like lashes out in front of us. Time ran out in Chadron because we had to make it to Helena by that night, and it was over 600 miles to ride north.

The road to Hot Springs resembled little I remembered. Even the big hill coming down into Chadron flattened. There must have been a reason for that, most likely, our leaving town, not our coming into it. In my reminiscence the first one to see the lights of Chadron yelled, "I s-e-e Chadron, I s-e-e Chadron." After our swimming trips to Evans' hot springs it was usually toward dark when we came home. No doubt, the plateau dropped out from under us, and there was the sparkly little town. Always it was a contest as to who saw Chadron first, and we all vied for first place. Competition abounded when it came to seeing Chadron first. That's the reason I know there was a big hill coming down into town.

We drove north passing the road to Pine Ridge Reservation. The road was taking us deeper into Sioux Nation country: the Black Hills: sacred ground. The sun warmed the morning, and as we approached the high prairie the grass began reaching in astonishing revelry toward the sky. Here is where it was the highest I'd seen it along the journey. I had talked over the counter of one of my retail jobs back home to a young woman who was a grass scientist. She was moving to Rapid City where she would continue in her grass research. I told her about this area between Chadron and the

Black Hills. She talked about the species and classification of grasses. Of course I dreamily talked of its beauty, and "Oh, the height. It must be six feet tall in some places." She began orating about what the Great Plains' grasses were like before the frontier was settled. Drifting in her description I saw the dresses on the wall across the room transform into monstrous swishing grasses. Then I saw the faces of two oxen appear through the grass as if through a stage curtain. For a moment there was grass and straight up there was sky. She yanked me back with "They don't exist anymore." How can miles upon endless miles of wild grasses not exist anymore, except in little pockets in the mid-west? Marg and I were dumbfounded by the mere possibility. As we watched the last remnants of that powerful genetic heritage pass by we realized we were driving through the lost vesture of The Great American Plains.

The earth began to lose its valley soil and the geology changed to rich red clay colored by iron oxide. The banks along the road looked as if our Creator had provided enough ochre for billions of ladies lips. We drove along at a much quieter pace. The end of the trip was in sight, and for this reason alone we lost our hurry. This morning we pushed the accelerator in slow motion. As we approached the town of Hot Springs, off to our left were vast lands of grasses which were part of Buffalo Gap National Grassland.

Marg and I grieved the lost grasses. In our sadness we began to bemoan the loss of the buffalo too. The mere mention of how we remembered having to wait for buffalo to cross the road on this exact road forty years ago fouled my mood. Quickly, my grief turned to anger. I started bitching loudly when we came around a curve and nearly mowed down a patch of unfenced bison. WHAT? Then we just laughed our guts out.

There they were a herd on both sides of the pavement. Little ones were curled up lying in the flattened grass while their mothers stood motionless against the hillside chewing juicy stalks of timothy. "Wow!" we sputtered, "Just like the old days." This was just short of a miracle! We'd heard the herds were gone forever, but now, here, this small remnant inspired us to wild outbursts of Sterling howling. Marg says, rather facetiously between trailing yips and howls, "They're WILD Kath, like us, whoop, whoop!!"

It was wonderful to pretend these animals belonged to no one, not a rancher, South Dakota, nor the federal government, but to themselves. They weren't worried about anything, not even the increasing number of travelers on the highway, but into another laid back day in the sun on the high prairie. The flies on their backs were as unnoticed as the license plates on the cars that swept past them. It was then that we created our horse Brownie. Margie told me, "Hey let's ride double on a horse just like in the old days. We need a horse to adventure out here in Indian and buffalo country." Any horse that we saw that was one color, white, black, brown yellow we named Whitey, Brownie, Blackie, or Goldie. Brownie from that day forward became our make-believe companion that would take us on many adventures in our future, and through Marg's illness finding answers in unusual ways. Brownie was created in *SACRED COUNTRY* like he just dropped down out of the Black Hills and there he was with us from there on out. We jabbered along feeling high as high could be. There was no thought of illness or the future.

It was Evans plunge in Hot Springs where our parents took us to face our fears about water. We arrived in Hot Springs mid-to-late morning. The county had torn up the road pretty bad, right down to the red clay in some places. We'd inched our way along in a long growing collection of mobile homes and campers. Where did all the people come from? There was only one road into Hot Springs and suddenly Highway 385 was bumper to bumper. We drove through the completely unrecognizable town of Hot Springs; as we curved left, then right the road cruised by a big building with a large red front on it. There it was, Evans plunge.

In the old days it was gargantuan. To little girls its breadth and height was as massive as an ocean liner. Its water sloshed about as swimmers dove and jumped into the deep end. There were trapeze rings suspended from the ceiling and only the expert gymnasts could swing them far enough to let go and hook up with the next ring in line. The plunge might as well have been Barnum and Bailey's circus as its roof jutted upward like a Big Top. We scampered about wanting to run in all directions, but under the watchful eye of our parents were halted from slipping and sliding on the concrete floor to our doom.

The deep end was so wide it would take at least six rings to get across it by air. To swim it meant you had to be really good because if you couldn't make it no one might even notice you until it was too late. I think it was a "Swim at Your Own Risk" kind of affair back then, so our dad was the lifeguard in the deep end and mother guarded us in the shallow.

This was back when our father was a father. He stood in the five-foot zone about three to four feet from the side of the pool. We all lined up and made ready to run full speed into the air righteously trusting Dad's long-extended arms. Often, he would dunk us under if we were the braver ones. The other's he held high to his chest after they splashed in. Dad was our pal. We usually tagged along with him when we could. He was immersed in our family life, and even had much time to spend with us, back then. We jumped and jumped, got totally saturated with hours of water play, and usually had achieved some new bravery or another by the time to go home. In the shallow end, which really wasn't so shallow, I'd walk on tippy-toes to keep my face out of the water. Once again, as in Chadron State Park, the shallow end was separated from the deep end with a solitary concrete wall shaped in an L. At one place in the wall there was a hole almost at the bottom for the water to flow through. I'll never forget the story of the fat kid that tried to swim through the hole and got stuck. Of course he drowned. That hole never did get closed, so it makes me think it was only a story, but all we had to do was take a look underwater with our eyes open and be totally convinced it happened, and could happen to us if we ever tried it. It was great for threats to the little sisters; we'd stuff 'em in it if they splashed us. As mother sat on the steps overseeing her brood we swam and swam, like tadpoles in a pond. She must have been happy because her smile and cheers bounced around the walls of that huge plunge.

Marg and I didn't dare go in for fear of disappointment the plunge would be completely changed. By its look on the outside there was no doubt the original was torn down and replaced by something modern: functional, but homogeneous. We didn't check for sure, probably a mistake. We inched on in the line of cars and campers paying tribute by looking in the rear view to see the barn-red building tucked into the red clay hill. The blue of the sky was gaining in brilliance and we drove out of Hot Springs.

I kept getting a distinct feeling we were coming into La Loba country for surely she would come here. The Black Hills, I'd heard in the news, that in the early seventies to maybe eight or ten years later some group led by Russell Means was retaking those sacred Hills. They were building a ranch for Lakota people there. Whites, on both sides were getting excited, those who despised the thought of Indian's exercising their native rights, and for those aligning themselves with Native spirituality seeking the vision pits and holy experiences since their own religions had grown weak and pitted with hypocrisy.

The Black Hills was getting a lot of press, and Margie and I only had our childhood memories of hunting for mica with its mysterious layers of shiny metallic skin. Maybe it was because our father believed the old medicine man from Pine Ridge, but we always had the impression the Hills were different from any others. Mt. Rushmore was a spectacle, but on any given day one could stand on the observation point with few sightseers. If anything our tribe of six little girls and our parents was the crowd.

Today, still the 4th of July produced more people caravanning their way along that two-lane highway into the Hills. It was slow moving. I wanted to get out of the car numerous times and hike on into the trees to just see if I could find a big chunk of mica, but if we fell out of line the exasperation to get back in would have superseded the joy of getting mica, and who could guarantee that. Just looking at the crowds I doubt there was one remaining piece still left on the planet. I found out later I could buy one at a rock stand along the road.

The convoy crept along as we wound our way up through the hills. When we came in sight of the signs to Mt. Rushmore we entertained, for one minute, to go stand on the observation point and view one more time, in twenty years, those giant precedent faces. As we came around the curve to Mt. Rushmore's parking lot we saw cars, campers, and trailers strung along on both sides of the road. The parking lot was full to overflowing, and it spilled out of the entrance like jellybeans out of a jar.

Even if we wanted to see the *Faces,* we couldn't. We lost a few determined tourists out of the line. After all they traveled all this way, and now they couldn't get in? I don't think so. I understood their position. Those travel RVs get about six miles to the gallon, a sad and ordinary truth these days.

It wasn't just the hoards of people that got to us, but the increasing pain of billboards which began popping up on the hillsides and along the road out. The sacred Hills of the Sioux and native peoples were junked, and I mean junked.
I felt sick. A wave of claustrophobia struck at my insides. All we wanted to do was run full throttle out of the Black Hills. Ghosts from an earlier time couldn't beckon us to stay. Even La Loba's presence wouldn't make us want to stay, and I

thought if she were here trying to gather up bones from these hills she would have scratched long and hard at the doors of silver mines that had collapsed long ago from the sheer weight of the automobiles, trucks, people and billboards. Had she wanted to free the bones from under the earth she would find it useless, and eventually would leave to find country that might render its skeletons to her more freely? Before two hours had passed Marg and I broke from the chain of traffic and began to pick up speed to the high plateau that bordered those sacred hills.

We drove through Rapid City, but this time not stopping, for the day was lengthening and we had Helena to make by midnight. The sun was beginning to drift to the west as we caught I-90. The great expanse of this country spread out before us. It was still late spring here, even though it was July 4th. After experiencing the heat wave in Illinois I thought maybe summer had come to South Dakota. In the place of prairie lupine we might find daisies and wild columbine this week, but it had only been a week!

As we followed the highway into Wyoming I remembered a freezing cold winter some ten years before when I had made this trek back from Oconomowoc to Montana. The van my family and I were riding in froze up just driving down the freeway. We had to get a piece of cardboard and stick it between the grill and the radiator to keep the water from freezing. It was so cold vapor from our breath hung frozen in the air as my husband jimmied the cardboard into that narrow space between the grill and the radiator. Metal isn't just cold at temperatures like that it's hot. Hot enough to burn the skin on your fingers.

As Marg and I drove into the warmth of the sun I looked out my side window at the fence line seeing what I remembered there on that icy ride ten years ago. Hundreds of antelope walked single file along that same fence-line for what seemed like miles. They doggedly thrust one fragile leg in front of the other pushing ever onward, to where I had no idea. I wondered how they could survive this cold, and I wished I could give them the heat I was sharing with my baby son who was lying snugly in blankets against my warm flesh as he dozed, his lips slackened around my nipple. This memory faded as the snow on the fence posts turned into meadowlarks warbling their sweet prairie song.

We'd filled Pearl up in Chadron. Having passed through Gillette the gas gauge was falling quickly. What did we have left in miles to Sheridan? I was driving so Margie looked at the map. At least fifty, she said. The yellow gaslight started to blink on and off for at least ten miles. Every time it came on I'd get tense. The whole trip we hadn't let the gas get so low. It must have been that flurried trip out of the Black Hills. We kept thinking, well maybe there was some gas station that would appear on the horizon, but no Texaco appeared to relieve our growing worry that we'd be standing on the side of the road thumbing into Sheridan.

Eventually, the yellow light just came on and kept us company. We kept on encouraging Pearl to stay with us. Where was La Loba at a time like this? She could have called up a tailwind for us. I don't know why I did it, but instead of driving fifty miles an hour (to conserve gas) I stepped on the throttle to get us there quicker, made sense to me. Well, not exactly, what sense is there in running out of gas quicker? I just wanted to get home, to get Margie home.

She saw home, too. Her feelings for home were not my feelings for home. I caught a glimpse of her expression as I bore down upon my mission. She was chewing on it. She might be thinking home? "Hell, then what? Take a left at the next tumbleweed. Head south. Get out of town. Hit the road. Go over the mountain. Get Brownie. Hightail it out a here. Hurry!"

But my sense of urgency kept the tires humming; that cranky yellow light was with us for forty miles, then we saw the familiar mountains around Sheridan. With relief I turned my attention toward the sky around the Big Horns. Thunderheads were brewing like black tropical coffee. Amidst the plumes of cumulous clouds blue-sky spun threads of ozone to layer the atmosphere in a mystical cloth. It was then I knew the yellow light wasn't going to get any yellower and that we would pull into a gas station on the East Side of Sheridan. Off in the distance we saw signs of signs and with a shout of glee I snapped the silenced strain. The work out of psychically pushing Pearl forward at eighty miles an hour for the last fifty miles was over.

We got out at the *You Save* gas pumps, let Pearl glug to her heart's content, cleaned the windshield, got a drink, visited the lady's room, and piled back in to strike for Montana. The wind had shifted. What had been a perfect blue day began to fill with the expectation of lightning, thunder, and rain.

Eight

Wyoming State Highway 14 disappeared into urban Sheridan. Sheridan's main street looked like the Old West's cowboy and ranching center. The Bighorns reached for the sky behind town like a gunfighter who'd been outdrawn. All kinds of western architecture adorned the hub. A bucking horse on a bar sign, cedar store fronts, and an old hotel with a saloon still stood intact. A quick look-see, as we drove through town, gave us the impression we were back in time, not a hundred years, but more like thirty. Progress was indeed western, and that I was grateful for.

We didn't stay long, didn't even eat, but drove through Sheridan, took it in, and pushed Pearl into La Loba Country. It was as if the storm rushed upon us as high current winds sped us along as if we were on the wings of a soaring bird. As the engine revved we tumbled along down the highway. As we approached the Montana border I kept thinking about La Loba. She was here, in these parts. I could smell her. I searched each rise for her, knowing that we were entering into familiar territory, and we'd be reaching home sometime tonight. We came upon the border, back to the direct root upon which La Loba first showed herself in the bones of the calf.

My god how summer had *not* risen to the occasion but it stubbornly refused to be born this year. Spring is eternal I know, but the warmth of summer must come, mustn't it? Lupines in mid-July? I suppose, for it had been an extraordinary year. The road pavement was smooth and dry. It stretched out toward Billings like it had been there for millennium, always smooth and perfect. The constant whir of the engine covered any howling we might have heard. We passed right by our pee spot

177

where I found the bones. We flew by without so much as a nod, or prayer, as if we lost our hope for summer. We spurred by, forgetting to bow down to the birthplace of our mother's healing. My pat fear, not requesting, did not stop here again.

As we drove the most glorious storm was building. Perhaps it began as a spring storm, with its chill hanging in the upper elevations and then changing to summer in an instant in a thunderstorm with lightening and thunder and hail. Billings went by with nary a glance to the right or the left. Industry is Billings. We saw it more from habit than from sight. We tumbled smoothly down the freeway. Helena was powerfully pulling, and we were caught up in an expansive wake like we'd been following an ocean liner through the shallows.

By the time we pressed through Laurel, the storm had split into thunderstorms. The Crazy Mountains were laden with lightening, and blackness engulfed her peaks. If I heard any howling I heard the crazy woman the peaks were named. For her loss was too much, her children killed, her husband murdered by Indians seven decades before. She chose grief without end, loneliness without party, fear, without relief. The Indians knew her insanity was great power leaving her alone and in some cases helping her. The peaks are called Crazies to this day.

The beauty of that storm on the Crazies lingered, gathering more and more upsweeping thunderheads.

Marg and I knew we were in for rain, but when? It didn't come passing the Crazies. We strode on into Bozeman country. If it had been winter those storms would have made Bozeman Pass impassible, but that day it was only doused with light raindrops. The green of spring erupted from the branch-ends of Doug and grand firs that smothered the Pass sides. This storm gathered its powers as we passed through the highest elevation. Rain began to drop in abundance, yet for some meteorological reason there were no cloud bursts. The tension stayed in a glorious way for as we began our descent into Bozeman the view of the valley lit a golden path through the Absaroka Range where all hell was breaking loose. Golden sunset rays manipulated the precipitation. It glowed like the rays from God's face.

We didn't stay on the mountain, for our road passed through the valley. God didn't stop us, for we were pulled out of the great chaos to descend into the sweet-smelling hay fields. We sat driving in silence into a brilliant sunset, which spread itself over three mountain ranges. The cloud formations on each range spun its own psychedelic picture. Our mortal eyes moved from one range to the next, a three hundred and sixty degree sunset. The storm had moved through the valley before we came on it. Fresh hay-on-rain is a perfume no one can bottle. We sniffed it like oxygen starved organisms.

We uttered short hay-drugged phrases like, "smell, look, oo-h-h-h". Then the sun began to collapse into the storm clouds along the horizon. As the evening forced the sun's brilliance to dull on the mountains we turned north to Townsend. Helena was only about ninety miles away now. I plugged in Willie for the silenced curtain-fall, as it approached. We let his gentle voice bring down the shadows as we moved into the night. I remember a hush, like at Flathead during the last hymn *Now the Day is Over* at the campfire. The melancholy tune in minor rolled over the words: v. 1 *Now the day is over, night is drawing nigh; shadows of the evening steal across the sky* and v. 2 *Now the darkness gathers, stars begin to peep, birds and beasts and flowers soon will be asleep.*

Seduced by silence we rode into the black wet night.

Soon, the on-coming headlights of cars were absorbed in our quiet. Willie crooned.

Then, off in the distance we saw a very small bright explosion on the horizon. It was so far away we couldn't figure out what it was at first. Then another came, and another, and another. We both sat up straight moved our faces two inches closer to the windshield and watched for another. In that flash we realized Helena was blowing off fireworks. It was the Fourth of July and we were arriving home, in the middle of a wet asphalt-blackened night, to a blast of celebration.

The fireworks burst higher in the sky as we clicked away the miles. We crossed over the viaduct from East Helena. Cars were packed against the roadsides as if they had followed us from the Black Hills. We carefully passed over, and drove down into Helena. Our journey to heal our mother of pneumonia had circled us back home.

That night we stayed with our friend Holly. We didn't tell her about Margie's diagnoses because she was fighting breast cancer, but as we slipped between the queen-sized soft clean sheets, Margie turned her back to me once again. I gave her what she wanted, a loving rub of tense shoulder muscles. The events of our time together on the road reverberated through our soul-spirit and when we were finally able to sleep, I dreamed of La Loba singing a new song over my sister and me. Holly was in the next room.

TRYPTICH

Journey with Margie

Margaret's Pearl

Final Resting Place

i.

Journey with Margie

In loving memories of my sister Margie,
a companion on the road of life.

And the saddle was shifting, loosening and making its way up the horse's neck as the steep decline of the trail took a switchback. Gosh, why was the horse's neck getting shorter, when all of a sudden the saddle slipped over to the side? He must have held his breath when I cinched him up. Horses play that trick on you, and I guess I fell for it because I found myself falling out of the saddle onto my shoulder on the rocky trail. He no doubt thought me an idiot because he stopped in mid-step and rather lackadaisically turned to look at what I'd gotten myself into. He probably thought, and she's going to ride me on the cattle drive? Once I'd got the saddle back on and cinched up tightly we were back on the trail. The hired hands made sure I wasn't going to "meet ground" again. It was expected that I saddle up my horse by myself, but they made sure to give the gelding a bit of a kick in the ribs to be certain he let out all the air in his lungs. The hand kicked while I yanked on the cinch. When we got the problem fixed, we continued the long winding journey to the bottom of the mountain where Hidden Lake lay secreted among pine and fir forests. It was deep, and somebody told the story of the man who decided to swim it on horseback. They never discovered the bodies because the lake was so deep they never could find the bottom of it. The light that glinted off the blue reflection of the bright mid-day sky gave the impression that nothing bad could happen here. The lake lay wide and round and on one side rocky cliffs jutted from the water's edge. Shale once slid down the mountainside like a kid on a park slide. It was the kind of rock that made for great chase scenes in cowboy movies, robbers running from the law shooting from behind rocks and sliding, moving rock as they tried desperately to get to safety.

The afternoon was hot and dry, and the horseflies that tortured the horses mistook us for them and took great chunks out of our legs and necks and arms. The only relief was to take our mounts, get rid of the saddle and ride them into the water. My twelve-year old frame and weight was small as it was, but as the buoyancy of the water lifted my horse in the weightlessness he made no notice at all that somebody was riding him. At first he felt the cool water as a large branch to scoop off those damn flies when all of a sudden he's walked out far enough to not see the fallen log lying in the mud at the bottom of the lake. His front foot caught on the log. He fell forward putting his head underwater. Panicking he came up as if shocked with electricity. There was nothing but a little piece of his mane that let me grip but soon that was like grasping at seaweed. I was in the water thrashing to get away from the frightened horse. Once he found his footing he backed toward the bank that had by now turned to a muddy pit of horse imprints. I crawled out of the water onto the mud bank. Both my horse and I were dripping with realization that as gorgeous as this hidden lake was it held some secret darkness. We cared no longer that the flies were back and nipping.

****

We rode Brownie. I was in front and Margaret in back. We rode bareback and had decided to ride with a hackamore because we were on a very special mission and didn't want a bit bothering Brownie. We planned to journey to the underworld and we knew that Brownie, in order for him to take us would need all the freedom he could be allowed. He was a good horse, strong, honest, and true. My sister and I had ridden him throughout our lives and knew that we could not make this journey on any other horse. Brownie was a mustang bay gelding. His breeding proved his status as a wild mustang and we were told he was free and ran feral on the plains of Wyoming. He put up with a lot from us, as we always wanted to ride double, and took him into some tight situations like the time we rode down the cow shoot at the Bar 9 ranch. He protected us when we were being foolish by not proceeding down a trail that showed fresh bear scat, and then there was the time that he refused to be coaxed to take the trail around the cliff. When we ran him full out he flared his nostrils, raised his head, and charged forward in the expectation that a wild herd was just over the next hill.

Today, we would be asking much of him for our journey to the underworld would take us to the bottom of Hidden Lake. I knew how to journey to the underworld because I had learned how to in a shamanism class where I had taken numerous journeys. First, a question must be asked before you were to find a place to descend. I had chosen a gopher hole once. As I jumped into the right little hole in the middle of a great field, the hold began to larger and steeper as my body picked up speed as I descended. I was sort of sliding uncontrollably to the bottom. I tumbled out of the hole, helter-skelter and landed rather dazed at the feet of a beautiful grazing white mare. So I had journeyed before this day. Margie had not.

That question we were to ask had to be agreed upon as we were to be unified, as one person on this mission for and answer to our question. Or, some direction from our animal helper, whom I was convinced we were going to meet. Margaret had been suffering with ovarian cancer for six years, and she was weary with the horror that trip takes you on. Surgery after surgery, chemotherapies, procedures, pain killers, meds for this and for that, and of course the loss and dread, anxiety, and depression.

Brownie got a good talking to before we rode him to the twenty foot cliff overlooking the east side of Hidden Lake. This is where we decided to jump from, and Brownie needed to know what we would ask him to do. There were those times that he protected us from doing anything "foolish," but today he must raise himself to a mystical mustang and shed all responsibility for our safety. He must listen to our call, as we would not, could not proceed without his consent. I knew, he, nor we, would die, but would be given supernatural powers to endure the dive and swim through the depths of the lake that is said to have no bottom.

What lies ahead? Is this our question spirit animal? Is it too simple of a question, or is it too complex? Is it about living or dying, what mystery can you reveal to us? We are sisters, children, one dark, and one fair. She wears her jeans with the cowboy belt and a pretty green cotton shirt. Her Buster Brown hair cut frames her petite features and gives her that tom-boy look, one of sheer adventure for she lacks fear and is daring and brave. No matter what she faces she is always bold even when she's scared to death. Giving up, giving up, always giving in to that thrust that makes her rush off the cliff to dive headlong into the coldness of that high mount lake. Me, I'm with her so I can't be afraid even though I have journeyed before, and I'm riding in front today, but it's because she is with me and we're doing it together, today, like we have all of our lives. My honey-blond hair lies softly curled to the nape of my neck. I too have a pair of wranglers on and I'm wearing an old pair of cowboy boots that I got second hand from some boy that had outgrown them. I loved them, even if they pinched my little tow on my left foot. But never mind, they were real cowboy boots, and I love them. My little yellow blouse was accented with a cowboy scarf that had Dale Evans riding Buttermilk on it.

Here we are, we're riding Brownie to the cliff. We've already had our conference with him and he seems to understand that it is only he that can take us to the underworld at the bottom of Hidden Lake. He picks his steps precisely as he walks the narrow trail through the woods to the cliff. It is an extraordinary day. The sky is impenetrate blue, and the summer temperatures are in the lower seventies. No wind is blowing as the still leaves on the aspen and mountain elders whisper nothing to us. We step into a silence of beauty. Call it a peace. As Brownie reaches the summit of the cliff the three of us look down to the surface of the lake. It is dark and deep at this point. We see the light rocks along the edge, and then they seem to fall away as the water quickly turns dark green into black only a few feet out from the cliff. We are not afraid. There is no catching of breath or squeezing waste or mane. What is the question again? "What lies ahead?" Is that our questions? We linger only a moment and then agree, yes, this is the question? We gave Brownie a nudge in his sides he turned and looked back at us with a light in his eyes that I had never seen before. Without hesitation, he backed up against the sheer cliff wall and than thrust forward, half running, and half jumping over the narrow edge.

His body angled straight out parallel to the water far down below us. He then, tucked his head down and we began to fall in a perpendicular position. Margaret and I were laid out flat against his back as the dive was executed perfectly. We hit the water with great force, but the very second we submerged it was as if the impact was absorbed by the softest cushion of airy water. The sunlight penetrated at the surface and as we opened our eyes we saw shafts of sunbeams streaking through the green water. Bubbles surrounded us as we fell deeper and deeper. Brownie began to swim with strong persistent strokes. The light at the surface was quickly disappearing behind us, but we noticed that the air bubbles never left Brownie's hooves. They looked like strokes of crystal in a sea of green.

My hand holding his mane felt how cold the lake was. The darkening waters began turning to indigo as we swam deeper and deeper. Brownie gave great thrusts in his stride as he pushed the depths away. I could feel Margaret holding me around my waist. Or was it I being held in her arms? It appeared that there was no life here in the lake, but darkness, actualized by more darkness. We couldn't see so well, except for the silvery bubbles that continued to accompany us at Brownie's hooves. We had ridden for a long time when we saw a form ahead. It looked like a man riding a horse. He and the horse were skeletons. Could this be the man and the horse that drowned in the story? If it were shouldn't they be dissolved in the lake, or imbedded somewhere in its bottom? But no, this horse and rider were still coupled together, even in death. Or, at least it seemed that they should be dead, until I saw the rider give a kick to the animal's ribs and they both galloped off, bubbles pouring out from behind hooves. As they disappeared, the rider shot his hand up and made a "follow me gesture." Brownie turned his powerful chest toward the mere shadow of the man and his horse and continued to descend.

As if by announcement we saw a great gate, an entry into a place that had been hidden from human eyes. The gate was open and Brownie instinctively took us through it. We must have penetrated the lake's bottom because the water above hung over us like it was suspended and it held us as if we were in a cocoon. Brownie slowed to a trot and then abruptly stopped all together. Margaret slid off his rump and stepped under his belly. She wasn't afraid, but had seen something on the bottom that shone and glistened in the mud. She picked it up and raised her hand to show us. It was oyster with a pearl that was huge and carried the polish of years and years of making. The oyster wasn't all that large. How could such a small oyster make such a priceless pearl? Margaret sat down on a rock. She held the oyster with the pearl in her outstretched hand. I jumped off of Brownie and scanned the bottom for another possible treasure. I found nothing so I went to sit beside Margaret. Together, we surveyed the pearl. I began to reach for it, to feel it when said, "No, not yet." I held back when we heard a voice that came from the oyster. It told Margaret that the pearl was hers, and that the oyster had grown it for her. She had worked for centuries on the pearl. Through all the years of grinding sand that made that pearl, spinning, spinning that wonderful mucous around it to protect herself from its brash pain. The constant sands from boulders collapsing, breaking forth from, and crumbling into tiny grains of sand that still hurt were the oyster's life. She fought the boulders when they became sand. She mucoused herself away from

189

the pain, surrounding her with other oysters, but those could not take the sand away, for they had sand of their own. Many died from the sand, but not this oyster, Margaret's oyster. Here it had lain for eons working to protect her, to ease the pain of existence. She knew she had a work to do, but did not know for what or for whom. She did complain, don't get her wrong, and she told us that if we hadn't made the journey to the lake's bottom she would have given up and probably died. Then her work would be in vain because who else would ever journey to the bottom of Hidden Lake for an answer---no one except Margaret, her sister Kathy and Brownie.

The relief of the oyster was so great that she began to weep and her tears were a royal blue that poured out of her around the pearl. This crying caused the pearl to be dislodged from her soft body. It began to float upward just a millimeter off the soft pallet. She told Margaret to take her pearl as a gift for what lies ahead. She told her that all of her exhausting and hard work to cope with the pain of the sand was indeed worth her life. She said it wasn't sacrifice, but I think pain is always sacrifice, unless, of course it is turned into something of great price.

Margaret reached down to the little oyster and took the pearl between her index finger and thumb. She turned to show it to me. As I looked upon it, I saw into it. I saw that it was another world with the beauty of light I had never seen before. It beckoned both of us, as it was so incredibly beautiful. In it, I saw a figure sweep its perimeter, and then disappeared into its heart. It wasn't so much what I felt I saw, but rather how I felt when I saw it. My curiosity mixed with jubilation.

Margaret held the pearl in front of her eyes and moved it back and forth, back and forth. She motioned that I untie my scarf with Dale Evans on it, which I did. I handed it to her and she placed the pearl of great price into the scarf, twisted it up to form a little bag, and then tied it around her neck.

We both stood up and knew we could ascend now from Hidden Lake. Brownie looked back at us as I first helped Margaret up on Brownie's back, then she pulled me up. This time it was she who took the front. I sat snuggly behind her as Brownie turned toward the surface. His powerful gallop through the water had our hair flowing straight out behind us. As I looked back that great gate was closed. It disappeared into black. Up we rode through layers of freezing water. We saw nothing for a long time, until as we approached the surface, fish of all sizes and shapes appeared. The lake seemed to be teeming with life now, but Margie and I didn't say a word. We just ascended together with Brownie. He broke surface into a star specked night. When he swam to the shore we saw that we were old women.

II

MARGARET'S PEARL

I remember the figure that swept along the perimeter inside the great gray-green pearl that came from Margie's oyster. She had slid off Brownie's rump to the bed of Hidden Lake's bottom. We had ridden our horse Brownie to the bottom of the lake in Montana looking for an answer to our question, what lies ahead for Margaret? Hidden Lake is said to have no bottom, so after an hour's decent, or some length of time truthfully not noted she, Brownie, and I with the aide of our guide, the skeleton of the dead man and his horse were directed to an open gate where Brownie neatly rode through, then slowed to a trot and stopped on solid ground. This is when M saw something shiny in the mud.

It seems now to me, after a few years have passed since our journey to the bottom of the lake and after the recovery of this exquisite pearl that was made by Margie's oyster that I must return to the scene where

...we heard a voice that came from the oyster. It told Margaret that the pearl was hers, and that the oyster had grown it for her. She had worked for centuries on the pearl. Through all the years of grinding sand she made that pearl, spinning, that wonderful mucous around it to protect herself from its brash pain. The constant sands from boulders collapsing, breaking forth from, and crumbling into tiny grains of sand that still hurt were the oyster's life. She fought the boulders when they became sand. She mucoused herself away from the pain, surrounding her with other oysters, but those could not take the sand away, for they had sand of their own. Many died from the sand, but not this oyster, Margaret's oyster. Here it had lain for eons working to protect herself from the pain of her existence. She knew she had a work to do, but did not know for what or for whom. She did complain, don't get her wrong, and she told us that if we hadn't made this journey to the lake's bottom she would have given up and probably died. Then her work would be in vain because who else would ever journey to the bottom of Hidden Lake for an answer, no one except Margaret, her sister Kathy and Brownie. The relief of the oyster was so great that she began to weep and her tears were a royal blue that poured out of her around the pearl. This crying caused the pearl to be dislodged from her soft body. It began to float upward just a millimeter off the soft pallet. She told Margaret to take her pearl as a gift for what lies ahead. She told her that all of her exhausting and hard work to cope with the pain of the sand was indeed worth her life. She said it wasn't sacrifice, but I think pain is always sacrifice, unless, of course it is turned into something of great price. Margaret reached down to the little oyster and took the pearl between her index finger and thumb. She turned to show it to me...

And that is when I saw the figure sweep its perimeter. I remember feeling jubilant for some strange reason. I return to this scene once again after some time now. My sister has survived another few years with her cancer. Her pain has been a constant companion, always laying the table for discomfort, for limitations, for bravery, courage, and desire to hang on as long as possible to life which means her three girls, Jimmy, the family, the ocean, the sky, the warmth of a lovely day.

I say to her, "Marg what is it like today, any better."

"No, I feel crappy."

The next day, "How is today Marg."

She says, "The same as yesterday."

And I think about the little oyster that spent eons of time making her pearl. Has she become the oyster? Where is the pearl that was knotted safely up in my Dale Evans kerchief so long ago before we ascended from Hidden Lake on Brownie?

I asked her and she produced an old box. Inside was the yellow scarf tied in a knot. She strained to pull at the knot to loosen it. I leaned forward to help her. Relinquishing the scarf with the pearl inside she let me tug on the knot until it began to loosen and open. It had been tied up since our journey in the lake. I noticed a strand of dried lake weed hanging from it like an old umbilical cord. Soon the knot gave way and in a moment I saw the pearl couched safely in the cleft of the unknotted fabric. I asked her if she wanted to take it out the rest of the way. She gestured that I could lift the pearl out of its secret place, so I put my fingers around it and carefully lifted it out, like a newborn after the incision was made in the mother's womb

The pearl was a grayish green, so lovely and very large. I held it up to the light to survey it, Margie watching the while. I sat quietly, almost not breathing, but hoping to see the figure that had once teased me with such joy. The pearl held on to its secrets while I held it to the light waiting for a spell. When I didn't see anything come forward to me, I dropped my hand to my lap. Marg lay back in her bed and gathering strength asked me if I'd seen anything at all. I said, "Well, not yet anyway." She closed her eyes and rolled her head to the right side of her pillow. I could see she wanted to sleep, so I slowly drifted over to the big chair in the corner of the room. There I hunkered down with the pearl.

It lay in the very center of my hand. It felt cool and smooth. I began to hear the melody of a gentle Irish tune and finding my eyelids heavy I slumped into sleep.

It was a flicker of light, like a fire a long way off that caused me to stir. I remembered that same light way off on the horizon when M and I drove north through Townsend on our way back to Montana. First it was a very small explosion of light then it went dark, then another and another. She and I realized that of course, it was the Fourth of July and there out of a wet Montana night we figured that Helena was blowing off their celebration fireworks.

The light flicked like an agitated flame in a drafty room. I watched it keeping my eyes fixed on the dark waiting for it's pinpoint of rascally light. It must have flicked twenty times when suddenly it sort of cracked and splintered off to the edges of the pearl. As it bounced off the perimeter it just seemed to fill up the whole pearl with a fiery glow. If fire could be mist, this is how it appeared, like vapor, but warm and glowing. It began to part as if an apparition might be disturbing its substance, and in one flash a cloak-like fabric engorged the pearl. The fabric as if attached to a person walking moved with the motion then it vanished from sight and the warm fire glow engulfed the pearl once again.

I watched the glowy substance begin to shuffle and suddenly there before me was the clear figure of a woman. She was carrying a little girl baby. The child was about a year old and had dark eyes and soft brown hair. In earnest, she looked like a baby picture I had seen of M long ago. This woman was not the child's mother, but much greater. She radiated with the color of blue around her like a very deep aura. From her head to her toes she was bathed in blues, from indigo at her head to fairy-like shimmering light sky blue at her fingertips. She held the baby close to her breast all the while comforting her and looking straight into my eyes. I felt that I wanted to reach out to her and touch this beautiful baby all soft and glowing with the energy of life. I wanted to walk right into the pearl and climb into the arms of this great lady. I wanted her to shift the baby to her hip and let me cuddle close to her, but there was a thick barrier that was lighter than a veil of finest silk. She did not say anything to me, but gazed with great love upon me. She smiled and then looked down into the face of the baby that was nestled into her breast. She drew her long sleeved arm over the child to shield it and protect it, then turned and vanished into the glow of the pearl.

I awoke and looked down into my hand where the pearl had been nestled. It wasn't there. I turned to Margaret as she lay still in her sleep. Her hand was lightly clutching something as her fist rested upon her belly. There inside her hand was her pearl. It rested upon her abdomen, her greatest place of pain, and I heard her utter a quiet tune. A flush came to her cheeks and her soft brown eyes opened. She sat up and without pain walked from the room onto a warm sandy beach where she walked down to the water's edge, turned back blowing a kiss and disappeared into the salty mist.

iii.

FINAL RESTING PLACE

Margaret's death day came on November 12, 2006. She is interred at the bottom of the Atlantic Ocean off the coast of Miami, Florida. Her remains are mixed in concrete to form an artificial reef.

> Our family was painfully splintered like dry wood and if lit on fire would pop and crack and throw embers in all directions when Margie died. On this one summer day there were only four who rented a boat to take us to where X marks the spot of longitude and latitude on the surface of the water to visit her gravesite, pay homage and find some comfort. If I had x-ray vision I could look down into the layers of water, like Margaret and I witnessed as Brownie pushed away the depths to the bottom of Hidden Lake in Montana.
>
> Her reef was home to a variety of living creatures: clown fish, groupers, eels, shrimp, and jellyfish,

all swimming among the anemones and sponges. My daughter Ann took a challenge by the two fisherman boat crew to fish for mackerel. She caught ten, and how I viewed it from Margaret's eye on the bottom, was to look up and see a large school of mackerel surrounding a boat bobbing on the current. After we poured red rose petals and some of mother's ashes into the salt water, we sat in silence and felt the sun upon our skin. After it was time to head toward shore, the engine whirred and as we turned, a huge group of large pink jelly fish surfaced all around the boat. When I returned home, I curiously looked up the symbolic meaning of a jellyfish. Margaret had spoken sending us back with two words, *Acceptance and Faith.*

I have faith that my shamanic journeys, shared with my sister Margaret are the reason that she chose her final resting place at the bottom of the Atlantic Ocean.

Montana Adolescence

For Montana

Waves of alfalfa roll over me as I dive into the waste high grass. We play hide and seek in the field, just out of shouting distance from the main house. The summer sky is streaked with fleeting blue as it retreats off toward the mountain tops. The air is filled with electric ozone. It glows like florescent plankton that laps the side of a skiff. Great black clouds are consuming the sky and flash-dancing bolts of lightening way off in the distance strike jagged snakes along the horizon.

God it is good to be alive! To be a part of the innocent stirring deep within where storms and children meet, innocent, unhindered. Watery drops patiently sprinkle the dusk's dry grasses. The smell of the earth: root, stalk, leaf, and flower surround my nostrils. I lie close to the dark earth. She cradles me close to her dun-brown skin, fertile and dusky. Her worm-riddled, spider-spun perfume seduces me. I lie, quiet, hoping not to be found. I bury my nose, for a moment, against her as if smelling a freshly picked bouquet of carnations. The juicy green and lengthy stalks of alfalfa hide me well.

I hear someone push the grasses aside. Jon might be the one who stumbles on my hiding place. Please let Jon find me. I hold my breath and lie still as a bird with its heart pounding against the dry roots of the grass. I am ready for him. When he does find me he will trip and fall; his arms will fall across me, pinning me helplessly to the ground. Under his weight I will abandon the earth and will know the universe far beyond the black thunderclouds. Muffled drops begin to bend the alfalfa. The thunder grapples with the aspen on the edge of the field. It is almost dark and way off in the distance I hear the faint clang of the bell.

It is time to go in.

Made in the USA
Middletown, DE
29 July 2018